Praise for *The Girls are Good*

'Chilling, disturbing and utterly compelling. I couldn't put it down.'
Sarah Morgan, *Sunday Times* bestselling author of *The Christmas Escape*

'A tight, frightening story of friendship, rivalry and obsession, told in sparse and beautiful prose. Tense as the space between the uneven bars.'
Abigail Dean, author of *Girl A*

'What a book! A stunning and revealing look the world of elite gymnastics. An unforgettable debut.'
Jo Jakeman, author of *Sticks and Stones*

'Brilliant, immersive, page-turning.'
Gillian Stern, judge of The Lucy Cavendish College Fiction Prize

'Brutal and brilliant – I read it in one sitting.'
Harriet Tyce, author of *Blood Orange*

'Dark, disturbing, desperately sad – I was totally gripped. What an incredible setting for a novel – a glimpse into a wonderfully dangerous, screwed up world. I couldn't put it down.'
Cesca Major, author of *The Other Girl*

'Dark and memorably uncomfortable.'
Sofia Zinovieff, author of *Putney*

THE GIRLS ARE GOOD

Ilaria Bernardini is a writer and screenwriter. She is the author of nine novels, a graphic novel and two collections of short stories. Her novels *Faremo Foresta* and *The Portrait* were longlisted for Italy's prestigious Strega Prize. She has created TV shows, including *Ginnaste* and *Ballerini* (MTV) and has written for *Rolling Stone*, *Vogue*, *Vanity Fair* and *GQ*. *The Girls are Good* is based on her novel *Corpo Libero* which subsequently morphed into a cult reality show. The story is inspired by Bernardini's exclusive exposure to the world of gymnastics over the past decade. The book has been adapted into a six-part TV series by Indigo Film and was co-developed with the support of All 3Media International and the Creative Europe Media programme of the European Union.

THE GIRLS ARE GOOD

Ilaria Bernardini

HarperCollins*Publishers*

HarperCollins*Publishers*
1 London Bridge Street
London, SE1 9GF

www.harpercollins.co.uk

HarperCollins*Publishers*
1st Floor, Watermarque Building, Ringsend Road
Dublin 4, Ireland

Published by HarperCollins*Publishers* 2022

1

A catalogue record for this book
is available from the British Library

ISBN (HB): 978-0-00-850304-8
ISBN (TPB): 978-0-00-850305-5
ISBN (E): 978-0-00-850306-2

This novel is entirely a work of fiction.
The names, characters and incidents portrayed in it are
the work of the author's imagination. Any resemblance to
actual persons, living or dead, events or localities is
entirely coincidental.

Set in Sabon by Palimpsest Book Production Ltd, Falkirk, Stirlingshire

Printed and bound in the UK using
100% renewable electricity at CPI Group (UK) Ltd

MIX
Paper from
responsible sources
FSC™ C007454

This book is produced from independently certified FSC™ paper
to ensure responsible forest management.

For more information visit: www.harpercollins.co.uk/green

How long can music
override the pain?
She reaches for the playlist.

Diane di Prima

MONDAY

In seven days there will be a dead gymnast, yet this morning, as I open my eyes, everything looks the same. Then again, my life is a loop and everything always looks the same. My first alarm wakes me at five past six, the second one at ten past. I like the first one because there is the second, these five minutes are mine only. I think of nothing, I am nothing. They are the longest five minutes of my day. At ten past six I wake up properly, click my neck and stretch my arms, my hands, each finger. I get up and feel the carpet under my feet. It prickles, as usual. It isn't one of those soft carpets, like they have at Anna's house. Ours is cheap and beige, the cheapest colour with the exception of school grey. Dad says being poor is OK because we love each other and, as long as we have our love, nothing else matters. I always make sure to nod in agreement, otherwise he and Mum get even sadder and I'd feel both poor and mean.

1

I wash my way-too-red hair, check my way-too-many freckles in the mirror, get dressed, close my bag. I walk twice around the chair, zip up the fleece of my team tracksuit and check my way-too-many freckles again. I open the door, tap the knob twice, go down to the living room. Which is also the dining room, the TV room, the kitchen and my parents' room. I eat my cereal, drink my juice.

Mum gives me a kiss and says, 'We'll miss you' and 'Don't forget your passport.'

From the sofa bed, Dad says, 'See you in a week' and 'Break a leg, little mouse!'

We really do love each other. Even though Mum's eyes slant downwards and even though Dad looks more depressed than ever. I won't miss them. I never do, I never did, I never will. But I want to win for them, or at least qualify for the individual finals at this tournament so that maybe – thanks to me and my road to the Olympics – one day they can have their own bedroom. Or kitchen, at least. Then I could stop feeling guilty that sometimes when they come to watch me compete, I pretend I don't know them.

I'm now 15, I was only 4 when I started doing gymnastics. Back then, no one knew if I'd be good at it, or if I'd grow to be tall or short. I also had no idea that from the age of 10, it would mean I'd find myself training at seven o'clock in the morning before school. Then again from three to seven p.m., and that I'd have to be doing my homework during dinner, sleep, then get up the next morning, six days a week, to train again at seven and so on. I didn't know Sundays would forever be for competitions and that my days would be so repetitive. I didn't know that I'd end up liking how things repeat themselves.

At least, most of them. Even though training sessions and exercises don't really ever repeat themselves because even in repetition there's always change. And in a gymnast's life there's always change. Like today we're flying to Romania to compete. This is new.

And new is both scary and great.

I open the front door and our team's minibus is coming up the road. I cross the yard, feel the freezing cold pressing on my cheeks, my eyes tearing up in the wind. The sky is lower than usual. Just like my hair today feels redder than usual. Fire red. Or maybe more strawberry red. I wrap myself up in my scarf, then do it twice more, before getting on with life and all the movements it requires. Walking, sure. Being with other people. Breathing, smiling.

Praying I won't die.

Inside the bus, it's silent. None of my teammates look at me. Anna and Benedetta are asleep, Nadia and Carla just don't bother. Rachele, our coach, is smiling at me, though she always tries too hard. When smiling. When talking. When all things. I give her a little wave, then nod to the physiotherapist, Alex. Even from here I can smell his last drink. And just like every day over the last five years I can smell his cigarettes, then the smell of his cigarettes on my skin. The smell of him on my skin. And that's another thing I learned when I was 10.

'Slept well last night?' he says.

'Yes,' I say.

I imagine him with his wife, sleeping well despite the horror he is capable of. Maybe she hates his smell too. Maybe she too tries to rinse it off with water, alcohol, or by scratching her skin with her nails. Will he really only touch us while we look like kids, as Carla says? Or is this too a lie? It could mean that when I'm 16, or max

17, he'll stop, and that will be the only good thing about being older.

That, and being able to eat more.

The only empty seat is next to Nadia and Carla, so I sit there and we all say 'Hey.' It's a one-hour drive to the airport, then a three-hour flight from Italy to Romania, and I feel claustrophobic already. I tap the window twice, zip and unzip my fleece, count to a hundred. The others are streaming music through their phones, but I still use an old iPod that was handed down to me from the hair-dresser my mum cleans for. I have to switch it on and off a few times before it works. Nadia and Carla look at my dinosaur contraption, then they shut their eyes, at the same exact time. It's like I'm watching them in slow motion, a choreography they've rehearsed. There's also a sound for the movement of their super long eyelashes and that sound has an echo too.

Whatever Nadia and Carla do, even breathing, they always seem to do it together. Maybe even their heart-beats are synchronized. Maybe their names, both five letters, are part of a larger picture. Carla wears more make-up and skirts and Nadia is all tracksuit bottoms. One is blonde, the other one dark. But these differences were probably decided at planning stage, so they'd be a better pair.

The first time I met them, they were 8 years old. Before that I'd only seen them at the training camp but they never mixed with anyone else. They'd come to visit Rachele's club where I was training. Carla was already a prodigy. And famous for being in a TV advert in which she said to a boy the same age as her 'Look what I can do!' and launched herself into three roundoffs and a double back somersault. She landed, smiled, and sat down at the table to wolf down a cereal bar that was supposed to give her the energy to do that routine. The boy moved away, dejected, but Carla ran after him to give him a bar of his own and they were both happy.

I know she'll have spat out that cereal bar as soon as they'd cut the scene.

I remember thinking that I wanted to be her and how was it possible she could smile for the cameras so naturally after a double backflip with twist. Then I realized I was always trying to smile for the juries and for the coaches. And for Mum and Dad too.

We all looked fine, from the outside. We still do. Some of us are just better at faking it.

I select the playlist of my floor routine and put it on quietly, because I hate it when music hurts my ears. I follow the notes and visualize a move for each one of them – the front pike, the aerial cartwheel – then I imagine the tune without the singing. I visualize being full of grace in a double tucked back somersault and a front one, a tick-tock bending my back to make an upside-down V shape, before doing the split leap. If my mind helps me, if my body helps me, this week I'll add a triple twist, which I've been able to do quite well for a few months now. I imagine crying a single tear of satisfaction after it, and smiling to the jury.

Then, to the world.

I curl up on the seat, my back to Carla, and go to sleep. I can sleep anywhere – my mum taught me. Even as a small child, I could fall asleep under a desk while she cleaned offices, at the hairdresser's while she cleaned salons, and on overnight buses when we were coming back from one of her faraway jobs, no problem. I sleep immediately and deeply. I dream of nothing. I am nothing.

When I wake up, we are at the airport and Nadia and Carla are laughing at Rachele's bum, which they say is looking bigger and fatter and flabbier.

'I can see the cellulite holes from here,' Carla says.

'I can see them through her tracksuit,' Nadia confirms.

'I can see the plates of pasta and greasy sauce she ate. I can see it on her face too, her skin is as glossy as cheese. Can you smell the mozzarella?'

Nadia laughs. She always laughs when Carla's being mean. Or when Carla is being anything, really. She laughs and she adores her.

I follow them, making it look like I am not following them – they hate me when I'm too close, and I hate myself when I'm too close. So I walk almost alongside them but a step and a half behind. Carla is swaying her hips and her designer handbag, which is printed with large letters. Now she's going on about flirting with her teacher during a history test in school last week. She asked him if it really was important to know what diseases were around in the Middle Ages. 'Should we not,' she apparently said, 'worry about other things?' Then she tells Nadia that she blinked in a *very* explicit way.

I've been listening to Carla and Nadia for years now. I've heard them analyse the growth – or non-growth – of their boobs, my boobs, and scan every boy, every girl. I've heard them, one by one, go through their families' obsessions, anecdotes, and secrets. For years too I've seen Nadia staring at Carla in the shower, admiring her back handspring in the gym. Praising her. Loving her.

I know she loves her. We all know.

I also know that they pray a lot at Carla's house. They read the Bible at dinner and in bed, before going to sleep, then they read more Bible with their morning coffee. If they have lunch together, well then, more Bible will go with that lunch. It's because they read the Bible together with their morning coffee, or with their chicken at meals, that her parents decided to stop Carla from being in adverts. It was OK to be famous before God got into their lives. It was permitted. Now it is no longer the right way to Give Thanks for the Precious Talent and Gift Carla has been Given by Him.

'You are God's gymnastic angel,' they tell her.

And even if Carla mocks them, I wonder if some of that sentence has stuck with her. She does seem to believe in being one. This faith, together with being able to fly, must help her with not falling at the vault. At the bars. Or ever.

Nadia's mum is very different from all the other mums. She had her when she was our age and absolutely hadn't wanted to. She's only 29 now and she'd be cool with Nadia having a boy sleep over at her house. Nadia isn't interested in having a boy stay over but tells us so we can see what her mother is like, that she and Nadia deal with fun stuff, like love, affairs, sex, and how to end things with boyfriends without hurting them or yourself. She tells us so we can see that they talk. That she exists.

'Just don't make my mistake, girls,' her mum told us one of the few times we spent any time with her. 'No pregnancies before you are twenty. Or thirty, even. Having kids is a terrible idea.'

I looked at Nadia and wondered what she felt at the idea of being often mentioned in a warning that was about mistakes and terrible ideas.

At the airport, we are the shortest people in the queue for the low-cost flight, and Anna and Benedetta are the shortest of the shortest, here and maybe in the universe.

That's only partly the reason we hardly ever notice them. The other one is because they are so scared of everything they have chosen silence as a way of pretending not be here. Or to be alive. Or in danger. Carla has nicknamed Anna and Benedetta the Useless Ones. We used to only see them when we trained to get into the national team because they came from faraway clubs, and Carla always reminded us that theirs were poor people's clubs. For poor people's gymnasts. But then Rachele invited them to join our club, so here they are. Here they uselessly are. Carla also repeats that both the Useless Ones and the entire team of the boys at our club are a disgrace. The boys never even make it to the tournaments, and she says they should become waiters, carpenters, or disappear, disintegrate. Maybe die.

Rachele always defends both the boys and the Useless Ones.

'They are your valued teammates,' she tells Carla. 'You know very well that when they win, you win too.'

But as much as Rachele reminds us of this, Carla never lets it go. And, to be fair, they never win.

'Let's not overdo it, Coach,' Carla told Rachele last time. 'Benedetta, in spite of her spectacular anorexia, is an elephant on the balance beam. Anna's scared of the vault and when she does a floor exercise she looks at her feet. They're *so* pathetic! Why do you even let them compete with us?'

In the queue for our plane, like everywhere in the outside world, people stare. I guess we look weird, little people with over-muscular legs and very coiffed hair all trapped in our identical tracksuit tops. In the gym, I like our bodies, I cherish them, but here I feel misshapen. I'd like to have it written on my forehead: We are gymnasts.

In this sport, it's a great advantage to have short bodies like ours and grow super muscular legs! We don't want breasts! We don't want periods! It's OK to develop osteoporosis at 13 years old, we don't care about growing tall! The important thing is to win and for this body to be strong and not look pretty when we are queuing!

But these would be way too many words to fit on my forehead.

Rachele always says thank God we are built like this, thank God we are short with no boobs, and thank God very few of us have periods and we really must thank God for our bodies, so tiny yet so strong. Otherwise, we could not excel at this sport and be champions and carry gymnastics high like a flag of the nation's power and strength. That's why she-who-puts-on-weight is done for. She-who-grows-tall is done for. She-who-grows-boobs, done for, unless she can endure very tight wrapping. Our body is our most precious possession. That's also why we live and travel with a physio. And that's why we have daily sessions with him. In theory, the sessions are there to protect our most precious possession.

In reality, it's in there that it all gets broken.

'The girls are good,' Rachele will say when someone asks if we might want to eat a bit more, train a bit less, or if we're happy about this life of being called dogs or elephants or losers as we work and sweat and hurt through our routines.

'We are good,' we confirm. And we nod. And we smile.

In our country there are almost four thousand gymnasts at competitive level. Barely a dozen are as strong as us. Physically and mentally as strong as Carla? I think there are none. Maybe that's why she's able to never talk about Alex. And maybe that's why she is so combative. Our discipline consists of floor exercises set to music, the balance beam, vault, and asymmetric bars. We do all the exercises individually but we are scored as individuals and as a team. It's an Olympic sport and it's the national team and the Olympics that we are aiming for. That is why Carla and Nadia moved to the North with their families and took up training at my gym. That is why Anna and Benedetta are trying to fit in too. Rachele is known as the best. She's also the toughest, OK, and we now know she's also a liar and covers things up, OK, but in her hands you get your closest shot at the Olympics. She has produced more gold medals than any other coach in this country. How many of them wanted to die, that we will never know.

'Be your best self,' she always says. 'Ask yourself if you want to be a prisoner of the past or a pioneer of the future.'

I wonder if she saw the sentence on a T-shirt. Or a meme online. I wonder if when she mentions the past, she thinks about the horrible past she knows we share. The horrible present she knows we share. And if that changes what kind of pioneers we could turn out to be in our future. I wonder if she thinks that as pioneers we will come back for vengeance. Or if she knows that we will be completely broken by then.

You do nothing for years but improve, jump higher, become more precise, more elegant. But as you get closer to turning 18, they tell us, you do nothing but get worse, weigh more. That moment is an ugly one, except it will mean getting rid of Alex and his fingers inside us and his smell on our skin. It's not even that far off. More or less three years to go until our decline. It's a bit like knowing when you'll die and that's a strange thing to know when you haven't even really lived yet. It might be useful, OK, because you have to make choices, like deciding how to spend the last days of your life, what to leave behind, what to be remembered for. And you have to take into account that although you think you can decide what you'll be remembered for, in the end, in gymnastics, or in life, it's not really your choice.

You might fall before. You might die before.

The tall girls for instance, even the great ones who get to competitive level, at some point they all disappear and for most of them it's a tragedy. What did those surplus centimetres have to do with them? They never asked for extra height, never wished to be taller. And yet their shin bones got longer, their shoulders more suited to swimming or weight-lifting. Their backs grew twice as wide as ours and, from behind, their backs were saying goodbye.

At least that's what they were saying to me, but I could never tell anyone because it would be weird, to explain about backs that are saying goodbye.

And then there's always Khorkina, the Russian who – despite sometimes insulting other gymnasts for being weak or moaners or bringing the power of God's punishments to quite a few sentences – gives all tall gymnasts hope. She is 1.65 metres, and is a constant reminder that, after being squeezed into bandages for years and after having been hungry for years, anything is possible. Even being tall and a supreme champion. Even being named *The Flamingo of Belgorod*. Even being beaten but thankful for it. If you want to achieve something, of course, as she says. If you want to be a pioneer.

At her last Olympics she had a black leotard, all made of Swarovski crystals. She named it her wedding leotard.

But there's one Khorkina every ten, twenty years and

11

in this ten, twenty years she's been the one, with exercises created especially for her, modified to fit her, so that even doing a twist with 1.65 metres to spin around can look elegant. Now those moves are part of the repertoire and are named after her, forever and ever. And when your name is repeated forever and ever in gyms across the world, somewhere inside you'll hear it and you'll feel it for sure. You'll feel someone is saying 'Khorkina' in China, or in a small gym in Spain, or maybe in Japan. Someone, while flying through the air in Canada, is mumbling, 'Now, I'm going to try the *Markelov-Khorkina* combination,' and that must be so beautiful.

Rachele is going over the away rules: mobile phones switched off in the gym, good manners when travelling and at the hotel. Responsibility and respect for our own bodies because each of our bodies is everyone's body. We must take care of our teammates and of our host country too. We must be polite. Smile. Say thank you.

Be good girls.

Looking at us from the outside, you wouldn't think that us teammates are also in competition with one another. Individually, each one of us has the potential to win her own event, to beat a teammate who's become an enemy. Nadia against Anna on the balance beam for example or Benedetta and I trying to better each other at the vault all the time. But there's no competing with Carla and you wouldn't even think of measuring yourself against her. And Nadia, who is second best, seems happy as she is. She seems, in general, happy for Carla to get what she wants.

'Don't even think of practising any romantic routines,' says Rachele, trying to be funny.

We don't find her funny. We find her gross. Carla mocks

her and makes the shape of Rachele's fringe with her hands, so stiff it could be made out of plaster. Once, after training, I saw Rachele blow-drying it with tons of hairspray. She was also lining her eyes with kohl and painting her mouth with a brown lip pencil to make an outline, filling it in with this thick paste. She was making herself look pretty but her eyes were teary. It might have been the black eyeliner or maybe it was because she knew that even if she put lipstick on, she was still lonely. And anyway, she knows way too many things that have happened to us, and to her, to ever be happy or pretty again. She is guilty. There's no amount of black eyeliner and orange lipstick to cover that up.

'She'll be sure to practise,' Carla whispers to Nadia, loud enough to make sure we can all hear. 'She'll do weird shit with some weird man she'll find in some weird Romanian bar.'

Carla starts making up her own rules.

'Rule number one thousand three hundred and six, respect the poor Romanians who are poor,' she says. 'Rule number one hundred thousand and seven, do not touch other girls' tits. Rule number two million three hundred, do not touch the boy gymnasts' dicks or, let's see, noses!'

We all laugh. At least we all do that sound that comes across as a laugh.

Rachele never gets too cross with Carla. She's our champion and this is why she gets away with everything. She gets away with a lot of things that we – who are good, but not champions – are forbidden to do. Be loud. Hurt others. Lie. We don't get cross with Carla either. At most we roll our eyes when she can't see us. Or we clench our jaws and grind our teeth.

We'd be nothing without her.

A downpour splatters the immense airport windows and a storm sets in. We all put our earphones back in – I choose a soundtrack for the storm – and wait for the time to pass, and the lightning to subside. Nadia's afraid of flying and she's turning pale. She has so many fears that we've lost count: falling off the asymmetric bars, being in the dark, being in lifts or locked in rooms of any kind, including public toilets. Loud noises and even very swift noises, like when someone whispers.

'They freak me out,' she says, 'like they'd bring bad luck.'

Carla always says that Nadia's half-poor but not really 'dog-poor like Martina'. And Nadia's always reminding us that if anyone knows anyone that needs a babysitter, she's free Saturday nights. Her house is very small – it's more like a room – and her dad's been gone right from the start. Her very young mum looks after very old people but only some of the time. She's trying to get a degree so she can earn more money.

'I need to repair my mistake,' she says.

Carla, on the other hand, is, according to her, 'half-rich' – which to me means very rich. Her family has a car, a scooter, two jobs, three bicycles and enough bedrooms for each one of them. They also eat meat at least three times a week. Or so we're told. They go on holiday to Sharm-el-Sheik or Djerba every two years, and in the summer they go to the seaside. If Carla wants, she can buy new skirts and T-shirts and doesn't have to wear her cousin's castoffs like me. Carla has an adopted brother, Ali, and she calls him 'my half Black half-brother'. To prove a point, because their parents are so religious, she says she doesn't believe in God at all at all at all, but we know she prays before going to sleep. And she always brings the Bible when we travel. We also know she loves Ali because when he comes to the competitions she hugs him a hundred times, saying, 'I love you, my half Black half-brother.'

'During thunderstorms it's possible for the fuselage to funnel the airstream so it hits the plane, usually without anything bad happening,' Nadia says.

'Did you really say *fuselage*? I'll never use the word fuselage in my whole life,' Carla says. 'You also said *funnel*. You're scaring me so be quiet, OK?'

When we're let on the plane we are the only ones on board who are sitting comfortably. The seats are so close together that people of regular height nearly have their knees in their mouths. I'm sitting next to a man who stinks of something like rotten fruit or rotten something and is reading the paper. He's stuck on the weather forecast page for the whole take-off, and spends at least twenty-seven minutes on the football page.

Maybe he too, by forecasting his life through the daily temperatures, is trying to be the pioneer of his future.

Nobody reads newspapers in my house. Mum likes the gossip mags she finds lying around the salon, but because she only works in the salon if someone is off sick, she very rarely gets any. Sometimes we go through them together and we laugh or comment on the love stories or the scoops on people we've never heard of. They get married. They have babies. They cheat. Get fat. Skinny. They shout and they cry. They die. Dad sometimes reads stuff about horses, the winners and the losers, and racing magazines so deadly boring the articles are about things like what's the best hay to feed your horse and the answer is always good-quality hay. He also gets puzzle magazines from his friend Nino's bar, usually already half done by someone else. I wouldn't be able to explain why our money situation is so bad or why we need to use things half used by someone else, T-shirts or puzzles. There must be a reason, but I don't know what it is. Once, I asked, and the answer I got was another question: 'You want something you don't have?' I could have answered with a list. I could have answered with a few drawings. But I said 'No' because that also felt true.

I didn't want anything I didn't have.

I turn off the used-by-someone-else iPod and look at the clouds outside. On the wings there's a shimmery dust, but maybe it's just in my eyes. The blue is bright and from here the sky looks like a safe place. Falling does not seem possible, and the thunderstorm is very far down below us. If I could, I'd stand on a wing, take a bow to the universe exactly like I bow to the judges, and launch myself into a never-ending succession of *Yurchenkos*. I'd love to land in some uncharted forest or island or river, with a perfect smile, my feet firm on the ground.

'I am Martina,' I would say. 'I am good, see?'

In the seat behind, Carla is reading a magazine questionnaire out loud. 'Are you the jealous type?' she asks Nadia. 'You're in a bar and a good-looking guy is watching you even though he's with another girl. What do you do? a) You look down. b) You look back at him. c) You go over to his girlfriend and tell her the boyfriend is a cheat.'

Nadia doesn't even get the time to answer before Carla is arguing with the questionnaire.

'How would you fucking know who he's sitting with?' she says. 'In the movies it's always his stupid dumb sister, put there on purpose to make you *think* she's his girlfriend. I'd definitely do this with my tongue.'

I can't see what Carla is doing with her tongue, but I can guess. Repetition. Loop.

Nadia laughs and says 'Gross' and 'Take your tongue off the window or you'll catch hepatitis, Ebola, malaria.'

'Rubbish!' Carla says and then adds, 'Anyway, talking about tongues, I kissed my next-door neighbour. The stoner. I wanted to give him a hand-job but got bored halfway through it.'

When I hear 'hand-job' I almost swallow my chewing-gum.

Carla pops up from behind the seat and shouts, 'Have you been listening properly, Martina? Are you spying on us, you snitch?' Nadia pops up too and smiles and doesn't say anything. 'Martina's getting horny!' Carla bursts out, and I go all red and worry that going red will really make it look like I am horny.

Which maybe I also am.

Meanwhile the rotten fruit man beside me is still poring over the pages of his newspaper, stuff about finance now, which he must find very interesting, at least as interesting as the temperature in Tokyo. After another hour or so, we start going down. I stick my earphones back into my ears and the first thing I see in this new world is the snow falling. I watch it turn the universe white, turn the land into a simpler map, all made out of black dots to be joined from one to ninety-nine to see what comes out at the end. Maybe a prize? And maybe my prize could be not to have to hear or speak to anyone anymore. I could stop talking completely, and everything would be easier. I'd become the girl who never speaks and in this new, easy role, I might even achieve some fame.

'How did it all begin?' they'll ask in the interviews.

'With the silence,' I'll answer.

The first thing I hear after the captain announces we've landed in Sibiu, Romania, and that the temperature outside is minus three, is Nadia laughing with relief. Carla starts with her evil parent-fed, TV-fed, shitty-people-fed theories again. According to her, Romania is sickeningly dirt-poor and Romania looks disgusting even through the window and even at the airport. If there's one place we could die on a plane, it's Romania. In Romania they eat dogs, they eat each other, they eat raw mouldy black potatoes thinking they're a delicacy. The Romanian gymnast Angelika has to die and we could stuff her mouth with tiny twigs, so she'd choke forever.

'I saw on YouTube that she's getting fat,' she says. 'She's a fat desperate ugly pisser of a gymnast. I'd like to spit in her eyes until she's blind.'

Nadia sometimes says that when Carla says these things, she really sees them happening, as if they were true. She looks at Carla to show her she is visualizing her words. She smiles, as if being able to visualize the ghosts of other people's words was a gift. But I don't think it's a gift and I don't think Nadia really likes to see the things Carla is talking about, as they are mostly disgusting and cruel enough to make you want to throw up or cry. I too have just seen the image of Angelika with spit dripping out of eyeless sockets, tiny twigs stuffed inside her mouth. I too have just seen her dead.

And now I don't know how to unsee it.

Once off the plane, we go through passport control. We collect our luggage and our first breath in this new white world is a mouthful of ice. In the time it takes us to wrap up in our hats and scarves, we're at the minibus. Waiting to share the ride with us is a gang from the national team's selectors who must have been on another flight or maybe they've walked all the way here and they started their hike months ago. We all say 'Hi.' Alex and Rachele get all formal, fake, and friendly, and we all cringe, just like when you see your parents trying to be funny or cool. Just like when you know that at home your parents shout and kick you and hate you but when someone shows up, they go all cuddly and lovable and that's even more painful than when they hit you on the head and in the stomach.

At least that is straightforward. At least you know what to do with that pain.

I zip my team jacket up and down again a few times, trying to make some order and sense of this day, of this new land. Carla takes a packet of Gummy Bears out of her pocket and shares them with Nadia who shoves a handful in her mouth. They check to see if anyone is looking and then chew and swallow. Maybe Nadia is treating herself for surviving the flight. Or for surviving Carla's words. I count to a hundred to stop craving those Gummy Bears and try instead to listen as Rachele goes through the roll-call of the athletes we need to watch out for, as well as our duties when we arrive at the hotel, and the timetable of our training sessions and competitions.

'Well, sort of hotel, more like a wartime vacation resort,' Carla says, having checked on Google.

'It's a classic one-week schedule,' Rachele continues, 'with training tomorrow and team qualifications the next day.'

The worst teams will leave then. Individual qualifications will be on Thursday and team finals after that. The event finals are on Saturday and, for those who make it, on Sunday there will be the individual All Around – where any qualifying gymnast will compete against all the others, on all the apparatuses. Only the best of us will make it to the All Around. We all want to get there, of course, but most of all we must want Carla to be on that podium.

One body, one heart.

The last thing Rachele says as we're going up the mountain roads, and just before getting to the wartime hotel, is: 'Carla, sit properly, we can see your knickers,' at which Carla blushes for about one second, during which I imagine Alex imagining those knickers. And ours.

But Carla has chosen to be Popeye.

'Seeing my knickers isn't a bad thing,' she replies. 'They have the days of the week on. Anna, do you want to check I'm wearing Monday? As you are already staring, you might want to make the most of your good eyesight.'

Anna wasn't staring so she doesn't keep on staring.

At the hotel, on the borders of the Cozia Forest, the rooms are already assigned and it turns out I have to share a triple with Carla and Nadia. Anna and Benedetta will think it's an undeserved treat, as sleeping in the same room as the champion is meant to be a privilege. But I feel nauseous just thinking that I'll have to be with them for six long days.

I'm used to being by myself and I like being by myself. I have never even asked my parents for a brother or a sister – not that we could feed anyone else. I've always thought it's better to be an only child. I even almost like our dinners for three, Mum, Dad and I, when we have nothing left to say and there's a silence, which I'm sure would seem sad from the outside. But I'd say it's a comfortable sort of silence, easy to curl up in. If we're silent when we're out in public though, having a picnic in the park or queuing for something and someone looks at us, then we immediately start talking, because we'd be ashamed if anyone thought we might be an unhappy family. And we smile. And I guess in some way we also bow.

In our rooms we unpack and pick beds. Well, I don't. I'm assigned mine, when Nadia and Carla push theirs together into a big double.

'I wish your mum was here to clean this shitty room,' Carla tells me even though the room is not dirty or messy at all.

'Your mum is adorable,' Nadia giggles. 'Like a soft, stuffed teddy bear. Adorable.'

'She is,' I say.

Or maybe I don't because I can't quite hear the sound of my own voice. I lie down on my back to check out how I feel, in this room of our new white universe, of our short-term brand-new life. I like short term and I like brand new. There are lots of beds in all the hotels, hostels, and bed and breakfasts of the world. I want to try them all and if I concentrate hard enough, even here, near this forest, I can see rain instead of snow outside this window, a tropical landscape instead of this white land. I can imagine lying down on a bed in Bangkok, and seeing Bangkok through the window. I do the same with Rio de Janeiro. Paris. I climb Kilimanjaro. I bow from there too.

'Don't drink the tap water,' Carla says. 'You can get a number of fatal diseases from it.'

We don't drink the tap water; we shower, watch TV, and put on clean clothes. Nadia checks her bruises and with a biro draws a circle around two she has on her thighs from last week's training. Rachele's been pushing her a lot and Nadia says she's grateful for that. We stare at her bruises. Then I stare at mine, comparing them, trying to feel grateful for the bruises too.

'These are record bruises,' Nadia says. 'They're sort of cute.'

We study the bruises some more and they're nothing we haven't seen before, and the longer we stare, the worse they look and something unspoken shifts between us, so we change the subject and chew one more Gummy Bear each. Mine tastes like watermelon. Or maybe peach.

Carla reminds us that in order not to put on weight, we should eat carbs only and exclusively before midday. Also, she says, as we are now 15 this is the ideal age to start having proper sex. She tells us she's discovered that to get our nipples to point out under our leotards all we have to do is stick a piece of Sellotape on them, then pull it off like a waxing strip.

She does it and shows us her nipples. They are in fact red and pointy. She also bets us that before the week is up, Rachele will make out with at least two rival coaches from different parts of the world, who the morning after will creep out of her room, shamefaced. And maybe Alex will bang her too.

'Vomit,' says Nadia.

'No shit,' says Carla.

We turn up the TV, I guess all trying to get rid of the image of Alex. I get distracted thanks to the Romanian music blaring out at top volume and I tune out until I hear Nadia ask Carla if she's seen the gymnastics accident on YouTube, the one where the girl falls on her head and doesn't move anymore.

'It says in the comments she died a month later,' she reads. 'But it also says she just retired.'

'So what?' Carla asks.

'Makes me cry,' Nadia says. But she is not crying at all.

'That's Romina Laudescu,' Carla says. 'She's alive and getting better. She's stopped competing and you should stop watching those things. Concentrate on yourself.'

'What's the point? I won't make it to the Olympics.'

'Don't talk crap. Of course you will.'

The truth is they will both make it to the Olympics, while I won't.

'Let's make a bet,' Carla says. 'If one of the ten first places at the All Around is yours, Nadia, I want to see you stark naked in the middle of the gym.'

'What?' Nadia laughs. 'OK!'

'Promise?'

'I promise.'

Later that night, as we queue for the buffet, I remember Carla's rule about carbs. It's way past midday so I get grilled chicken, white beans and a small bottle of water. At the end of the queue, Rachele examines my tray.

'Put those beans back, Marti,' she hisses. 'You'll end up with a bloated tummy.'

Like a good girl, I do as I'm told. I put back the beans and consider bowing but I don't.

As I sit down, Angelika makes her entrance. Since the last time we saw her at the Europeans, she's become even more striking. Angelika Ladeci, now 15 years old, with bright blonde hair, super tiny and with a perfect body, is joining her team, at the far end of this neonic room. The big bum Carla said she saw on YouTube is a total lie. She's half our size and we're already half the size of a normal person. She's stunning, obviously a champion, a multiple prize winner and ever so light. When she walks it's like there's music playing just for her. Her eyes are the perfect blue and her nose is as small as a baby's.

I hear Carla ask Nadia, 'You think she's beautiful, don't you? Well then, picture her having to eat dog food because she's a bitch among dogs. She's actually more revolting than the most revolting dogs. Then picture her sleeping on the floor because she doesn't even have a bed, not even a blanket, not even a mattress. She has to make her leotards out of tablecloths or curtains.'

Thinking of these things makes Angelika seem even more special to me, like Cinderella or Snow White. I even think about 'The Little Match Girl' and the other million stories in which very pretty, but above all, very unfortunate girls, manage to bring about nuclear change to their tragic destiny. I turn around and see Nadia's eyes have gone weird, like when she's seeing things. She is probably visualizing Angelika on all fours eating out of a bowl. Maybe she's imagining her covered in fur, with a smelly damp muzzle.

That's what I'm doing, anyway.

Later that night, my body aching from the absence of exercise, I get into bed so full of other people's words, I feel like I've been poisoned. Carla still has stuff to talk out and Nadia is laughing happily, listening to an explanation of how to give boys the kind of massage they like.

'Would you do it to Karl?' Carla asks.

'If you teach me,' Nadia answers. 'And if you want me to.'

I put my pillow over my head but the sound of their voices comes through, and with them the image of little Karl, the Polish athlete who has become the sex symbol of junior competitive gymnastics. I'm not in the mood to imagine Karl and massages so I ask them if they can keep it down and Carla says, 'You are so boring, Martina!' but then she switches to whispering, and with the pillow over my head I can barely hear anything anymore as I finally feel myself drift off.

In the middle of the night, I get up and tiptoe to the loo to pee.

I open the door, tap the knob twice with my fingers, then I tap it twice again to close it behind me. When I return to the room, I look at Carla and Nadia sleeping in each other's arms. On Carla's bedside table I see the Bible, and her painkillers.

Watching the girls breathe quietly, I have another flash of Alex, his bloodless knuckles, holding my ankle with one hand and touching me inside with his other hand. His breath. My breath. I wish I could find comfort in Carla and Nadia's arms too. Or should I try Carla's Bible? Maybe the painkillers. I go back to my bed and choose the usual method. I start counting to a hundred then to another hundred. I make it to a million.

'Help me,' I say. But nobody can hear me.

TUESDAY

'You bitch!'

I open my eyes and see Carla leaning out of the window, then hear water, and an image comes to me of Nadia under the shower, still charting her bruises. I pop the usual painkiller and stretch, feeling the stiffness and aches in my muscles. Today they are worse because I didn't train yesterday.

I say, 'I'm starving' and Carla turns around, startled.

'Oh, hi,' she says, 'I forgot you were here too. That bitch of an Angelika was training just under our window. What the fuck? You think she does it on purpose?'

I'm wounded she'd forgotten I was here, so invisible and irrelevant to her. At the same time the thought strikes me that I'm not at home, so can't eat double breakfast portions and instead will have to endure Rachele watching what I choose, weighing my cereal with her eyes.

I touch my nose twice, count to a hundred while I blink in repetitions of ten, pause, then do another five repetitions of ten.

'Get a grip,' says Carla. 'Stop doing that shit.'

'Leave her alone,' Nadia says. 'At least in here, when Rachele isn't watching.'

Rachele has been my coach for eight years, and for six years she's been on my case. Like when she insists on making me repeat every exercise twenty times even when I say my arms are so tired I can't hold them straight and she tells me I'm just lazy. When my arms give in and I end up bumping my chin or my shoulder on the mat, she sighs, like I'm worth nothing. Once I hit my nose so hard it bled.

A few years ago, we had a teammate, Caterina, whose mother was more in tune with what was going on at the gym than any of ours. True, Caterina suffered more fractures than the rest of us but then I think about the falls I have taken, my constant feeling of being about to snap in half, and I guess someone could have saved me too. All of us have suffered stress fractures but nobody has ever come to take us away.

Besides, I wouldn't have left. Nor would Carla or Nadia.

'Good girls,' Rachele always says when we don't complain and instead of crying we push ourselves so much we cut our palms, injure and bruise our bodies until we are layers of hurt. And we smile. We nod. And we bow.

I wait for Nadia to come out, then I get dressed in the bathroom. I don't want her or Carla to see me naked. Especially Carla. I can put up with being naked in the changing rooms, where I blend in with the others, but in the bedroom I'd be too visible.

Carla always has something to say about other people's bodies and she fixes her eyes on you without a trace of embarrassment and checks out disgusting stuff like pubic hair or cellulite or bulging veins. Once I even saw her sniff Anna and Benedetta's armpits, right up close to their skin.

'Dogs,' she whispered.

And Nadia had mimicked a dog, on all fours, barking.

When I come out of the bathroom, Carla and Nadia are sitting on the bed, fully dressed, their pulled-back hair buns almost identical, busy lacing up their trainers. They are picture perfect, so pretty you love them or hate them straightaway. Carla with her blonde hair, full lips slick with gloss, plump cheeks, and bright blue eyes. And Nadia, with her delicate hands despite her callouses, her long slim fingers, her slender neck.

Her hair, so curly and so dark.

'Do you remember that time you said you wanted to see wolves?' Carla says to her. 'We were at your house and we saw that film about the little girl who lived with them.'

'They protected her and killed for her. I loved those wolves.'

'Well, look out there.'

We press our noses to the window. I see the ground covered in snow and Angelika sprinting round in circles, near the low gate that separates the war-like hotel from the nothingness beyond. She looks so carefree, as if she doesn't have a worry in the world. But then again, it could be the distance.

Or it could be her being a good girl too.

It would be such fun to go and shake the trees and stand under the falling snow and stick my tongue out, I think. The cold down on our backs would make us laugh and we'd forget everything – all of our pain, all of our life – for a few seconds at least. But there are no wolves to be seen, and anyway we wouldn't be allowed to go out there and play.

'Where's the wolf?' Nadia asks.

'It vanished into the forest,' Carla says. 'Didn't you see it?'

'No,' says Nadia. 'Was it really there?'

I tap the window twice and they look at me.

'Sorry,' I say.

I wish I could stop doing things in sequences. And I wish I didn't make so many mistakes on the uneven bars. Or in life. I must have got it from Mum. Sometimes when she talks she makes stupid mistakes with her words. Or with the clothes she wears. She used to be pretty but now she hardly ever washes her hair. She usually does it on Sundays but by Tuesday she has to tie it back because it's already gone greasy. I haven't seen her naked for years now, but I remember she used to look great in her swim-suit. And perfect in her knickers and bras. And why doesn't Dad go out every morning to look for a job? He wants to be with us, he says, but I go to school, then gymnastics, and Mum works every day. He only smokes, goes to Nino's, does half-finished crosswords, and reads that stuff about horses. Who knows why they fell in love and how they managed to make me. Had it been down to them alone they wouldn't even have had the energy to complete my feet or DNA.

Stepping away from the window, I have to touch my hair twice and take two steps with my left foot and two with the right, before I can sit on the bed.

'That idiot goes running when it's zero degrees outside,' Carla says. 'She's going round and round in the snow.

Earlier, I saw her disappear into the forest wearing just a leotard and tracksuit bottoms. What a pathetic show-off!'

'She's been doing it every morning and every night forever,' says Nadia. 'I read it online. Her first coach taught her. That gross man Florin, who dropped dead of a heart attack when some of the girls accused him of hitting them.'

Their Florin, our Alex. Their man. Our man.

'She might get eaten by wolves,' Carla says. 'Or maybe because of the cold she'll get diarrhoea. Just when she's doing a floor routine, a proper bout!'

Carla starts to do an impression of Angelika getting a bout of diarrhoea during a handspring. She pretends to be Angelika greeting the jury, on the beam, sitting in a corner, having belly cramps. Angelika with diarrhoea and belly cramps has screwed-up eyes and her mouth is wide open. 'Ouch, ouch,' she moans. 'It hurts, it hurts!' Then, she puts a hand on her bum to hide the mess she's made.

'A bit like you, Martina, when Rachele gave you laxatives,' Carla says.

'You promised never to repeat that,' I say. 'You *promised*!'

They are both smiling.

'Just having a laugh!' Carla says. 'We love you so much, Marti.'

I try to take it as a joke, glad that Carla is smiling at me. To do so I press my nails into my palms. Then, in the thighs. As we leave the room, I tell myself, *Be happy. They love you. They love you so much. You too can love them so much.*

As the door slams behind us, we see Anna and Benedetta

coming out of their room. They are jolly and tidy. I envy their peace. I envy their room with no Carla inside.

'Morning, Useless Ones,' Carla says.

'We love you, girls,' Nadia adds. 'We love you *so* much.'

'We love you too,' they answer.

When the lift arrives, we find that a wall of Chinese girl gymnasts are inside it. We are so tiny we can all fit in, but coming across the Chinese team is always very scary. They scare us because they are strong and because they remind us that we aren't free, even if we pretend to be. So we roll our eyes and make a face. We don't want to meet their eyes as we think theirs are the eyes of loyal vassals, faithfully pleasing their own enemy. Just like ours, but more obvious. Carla says that Chinese gymnasts are like beaten dogs, or beaten poor dogs or beaten stunted dogs. What she doesn't mention – but we all know – is that we belong to the same pack. Carla uses the word dog at least one hundred times a day. And if she uses it ninety-eight times, Nadia will add the missing two to make it to a hundred. Or she will make the usual impression while barking on all fours.

Once we watched a documentary on YouTube about Chinese gymnasts and it made us cry. There were 5-year-old kids dangling by their arms, and their tiny bodies were crushed by the coaches, feet bound and hands shattered, to make it clear who was the boss and to what extent their life didn't matter. We watched it feeling gross and complicit, like when you watch porn, but this was way worse because we were in that movie too. It was also like watching real-life footage of nursery teachers slapping 10-month-old babies, and being those babies and feeling those same slaps.

We've also hated doing the splits, taking ice baths for

our muscles, and those coaches and physios who went way too far and tried to make our arms longer by pulling them over and over again. We hated them for calling us pigs and losers. Or dogs. We hated them when we tried to smile anyway. To be good anyway. And this is why we are afraid of the Chinese more than any other team. Looking at them is looking at what we cannot rebel against either. It's like looking at the most honest mirror.

When we reach the ground floor and the lift doors open, we exhale.

'Fucking robots,' Carla hisses.

'Weak animals,' Nadia adds.

We raise our chins towards the ceiling, adopt the gait of the confident team we know we are, winners at seven o'clock on this Tuesday morning in Romania, and walk into the hotel's canteen. The neon lights above us flicker in sync with our steps. A high-paced soundtrack would really work well now. We are a team – one body, one heart – and even if sometimes we forget, we have the ability to become it in an instant. Even though we have not chosen each other and we may not even like each other, we protect and look out for each other. We are the guardians of our collective memories and secrets. Of our childhoods and of our present. We know if we'll ever succeed in doing a *Yurchenko 2.5* at the vault or a double dismount on the balance beam, and how much we can endure before bursting into tears. We know what makes us angry or terrified. If we have our periods. If during a routine we are in the middle of a panic attack or in the middle of what we call the *twisties* – a mental block that makes us lose spatial awareness during a routine – which will eventually crush us. We know that when one of us scores a point, the whole team scores a point. And that Carla is the strongest part of our body. She knows it and we know it and this is why she's more precious than us and we take better care of her than of anyone else. We ache when she does, we have a temperature when she is feverish, and her weak left knee scares us as much as it scares her. When Alex touches Carla under her leotard, he is touching us under our leotards too. We can sense when it happens to her and I am sure she can sense when it happens to me. To Nadia. This is also why I can sense that the Useless Ones have been, for whatever reason, spared Alex's attentions. We also know that Carla has decided never to tell or say anything about any of it – 'Nothing would change,' she said – but she knows the exact words Nadia and I used when we told Rachele what Alex was doing to us. And nothing has in fact changed.

There's something icy about the canteen; the sub-zero temperature outside makes everything white and blue, electric blue and bright white. The light coming through the window slows down our hearts.

'Even Transylvania looks better covered in snow,' Carla says.

From what I have seen, Transylvania is beautiful. The forest, the emptiness, the maybe-wolves and the maybe-bears living out there. I could stay here forever, never go back to Mum and Dad. I could be a warrior in this other new Romanian life of strength and freedom. I could be a winner.

We pour ourselves some orange juice, drink our coffee, bite into one plain cardboard biscuit. Better it tastes grim, as it makes it less desirable.

'The towels here are so scratchy, what the heck?' Carla says to the Useless Ones. 'Have you noticed?'

They nod. We all do.

'They practically scraped my skin off,' Nadia adds.

'We should recommend them to the Polish girl with the yellow acne,' says Carla. 'If she rubs them on her face, the pus will come off.'

I suddenly realize I'm incredibly hungry, so hungry it's like being the whole world's hunger. I want to say it out loud: 'The whole world's hunger, that's me!' But over the years I've already come up with too many nonsense phrases. Like the time I said, 'When I'm on the uneven bars I feel like I'm between two galaxies.' Everyone went silent and at first I thought I was special and clever, that my friendless phase was over. I could open myself up to the world and everyone would admire me. And love my cute ideas on life. But they'd all laughed hard and inside I'd died of shame. What kind of dumb idea was that about galaxies, anyway? And what did it actually mean to be between one galaxy and another?

I keep silent while Carla comments on the Portuguese coach's bum, on the German athlete's boobs, and the French champion's eczema. Then she moves on to the Hairless Anorexic with Stinky French Breath of Stinky French Garlic.

'But the French are rich,' Carla adds. 'They can stink, as far as I'm concerned. You can't smell their breath in the huge frescoed rooms of their palaces.'

We all nod and say we only know Versailles from the TV, if that. None of us have ever been to France or seen a frescoed palace. And we've never tasted any French food either and the garlic thing is only something we heard – Carla included – about a million times from the cleaning lady who works at our gym.

'They're free to eat garlic, or rats even,' Carla continues. 'They will always have Paris. And the French R. And the money.'

Carla and Nadia are getting on my nerves and it feels as if my head is creaking with pain. I watch them while trying to hold my eyelids very still. I want them to understand how sorry I feel for them. But they never look at me, so I give up. The second Karl, the Polish champion, comes into the canteen, all the girls look up, or down, straightaway.

He really is handsome.

Hair slicked back with gel, square jaw and hooded top with the zip open. He queues with his little teammates then sits with them. We've watched Karl grow up and now all of a sudden he's turned into an Adonis. Does he have wings, too? To fly maybe with me to Bangkok? I wish our boys had made it to the tournament. They would at least have got us closer to the demigod.

All the girls, including us, resume chewing when Karl starts chewing. He is looking at Angelika, of course. Then at Carla, of course. Carla raises one eyebrow only and Nadia studies him without changing expression, sort of hypnotized.

'Beautiful,' she whispers.

'Well,' says Carla. 'He'd be perfect for an underwear advert.'

'He's grown at least twenty centimetres taller.'

'He's still a record-breaking dwarf though,' says Carla. '*Guinness Book of Records* stuff. Now can we please stop staring at him or do we want to look like total losers?'

We stop staring at him and looking like total losers. We walk to the gym in the snow and I study the trees, the colours, the temperature and try to come up with new details for my life here. I'll be a warrior and I'll have escaped all of my present and all of my past. I will choose a new name. Build a cabin. I will be able to hunt for food. And I will stop doing things twice.

'Move that arse,' Carla says to me.

I move my arse, we cross a bridge over a highway, walk further in the snow, and arrive at a vast building. Rachele lets us know that for the warm-up we are sharing the gym with the French, the English, and the Romanian squads. The other group will be turning with the Chinese, the Germans, and the Spanish. Tomorrow we will have the team qualifications, so now, she tells us, we'd better familiarize ourselves with the space, adjust to the apparatus and the atmosphere.

'We're sharing with the boys!' Nadia says. 'Karl forever!'

It's a proper, uber, mega gym. The floor and walls are painted in blue. It smells good, a mixture of lemon-scented detergent, clean air, and discipline. I like discipline and I like things to be tidy. And predictable. I suddenly feel so good I say, 'Karl forever!' But I say it so quietly I manage to make it sound like a cough.

Rachele shows us the section of gym we've been assigned. I can't wait for the warm-up, and all of today's training. My muscles feel like they're made of wood. We haven't used our bodies for at least forty hours and now we have to move them to bring them to life again. To make them happy again, and ours again, by warming them up. I'm always afraid that if I don't train I'll be punished and find myself incapacitated by a divine astral cosmic spell, as if I've been dreaming all this time and my efforts, the medals, and the days of gymnastics were never there.

'Please be back,' I whisper to my body. 'We're in Romania. We need to adjust. But you know all the same things you knew back home, OK?'

Alex rubs my muscles with some heated cream. I look at his hands, making sure he doesn't move upwards. His are hairy hands. With brown age spots. One of the spots looks like a star.

'Feeling ready, Martina?' he says.

I nod, imagine pulverizing the star, look away. I count to three hundred and he's on Anna's legs. He looks so focused. He looks so nice.

'Feeling ready, Anna?' he says.

I look at his hands, making sure he doesn't move them upwards on Anna either. Then I stand up, go near the uneven bars. Carla and Nadia say very quickly, 'Red red yellow blue – Coca-Cola Fanta glue – teeth straight feet straight – me me but it's you – blue pooh Fanta glue – I protect and so do you.'

They do it before every training session and before every competition. Back home the boys parrot the good luck rhyme to make fun of them, but with swearwords or only the part about blue pooh over and over. Nobody knows where their mantra comes from. Blue pooh. What's blue pooh, anyway?

We all start with a run. We go on to stretching, floor exercises, walkovers, handsprings. Kick walks, walks sideways, handstands. Rachele watches us move to the vault, then to the uneven bars. So does Alex.

'Creep,' Carla says, looking at him.

'Pig,' Nadia says.

'Good work!' he shouts from his corner.

I wonder if the other girls – just like me – are imagining him dead.

To feel our bodies breathe again, move, to welcome sweat on our chests and backs, is the best. Our movements get easier with every second, our legs more flexible with every step. Not training gives us backache and two weeks is long enough to see muscles turn into fat. We have watched an endless series of ex-gymnasts get chubby. It's one of our top three fears. Together with paralysis and never winning anything in our whole lives.

As we bend, jump, and land, we peek at the other teams. The Japanese club, the American one, the Hungarians. The French, the English, and the Romanian. Not all clubs will qualify today, and some will disappear tomorrow and have to leave Romania. We spy on their routines, scope out their weaknesses. We hate the pretty girls and admire the Romanian coach, Tania, who is much thinner and more stylish than our curvy Rachele.

'She's thin because she doesn't eat,' Carla explains. 'They no have money for food.'

'Their leotards are better than ours. And they are also allowed to wear shorts to train like the Germans. I hate spreading my legs without them on,' Anna says.

'Not wearing your shorts keeps you elegant and in shape,' says Carla. 'Don't moan.'

Sometimes I think Rachele and Carla have secret meetings to decide how to make us all obsessed with things like not wearing shorts during training or staying thin to not get our periods.

During another round of abs, Nadia starts talking about calamities like falling and fracturing our vertebrae. While we are stretching our legs, she tells us about that Chinese girl who died and the French one who was left paralysed and the Swede who is currently disappearing in hospital with anorexia.

We are used to hearing Nadia make lists, recounting accidents and updating the quadriplegic roll-call in gymnastics. She goes on about stuff like this because she's convinced that it's statistically impossible to end up paralysed if you talk out loud about the possibility of ending up paralysed.

I kind of trust her. Or again, the repetition has turned her superstition into a solid theory.

A couple of years ago, Nadia went as far as making charts and tables. She would sit with a notebook and pen, cataloguing the month's known accidents in order of seriousness, categorizing them by age, school, and region. It was so scary Rachele had to officially stop her. Nadia tried to make light of it.

'It's maths,' she protested. 'What's so bad about maths?'

Rachele's sanction was non-negotiable and the rest of us heaved a sigh of relief because it was impossible not to go through that notebook and fall into the same manic computation. But I think that it's surely worse seeing Rachele make the sign of the cross on her chest before we do our jumps or turns. Or hearing Carla and Nadia repeat their idiotic rhyme and having to wonder about blue pooh forever or seeing the boys touch their dicks eleven times before every jump at the vault. Then again, maybe we're all a bit obsessive. I have to do things twice, and sometimes even ten times in a row, and in the end we usually all turn a blind eye to each other's monsters and manias and we'll pretty much take any spell that we think will make us win and not die.

After an hour of warm-ups, when our bodies and our minds are strong and ours again, we start practising our competition routines. Floor routine first. Then beam. While we are working at the bars – our hands covered in chalk that will maybe one day leak right into our blood through cracks in our skin – other teams work on the rest of the apparatus. We rotate around the gym in shifts of thirty minutes. I am unsure and weak in every single section, the beam being the worst.

Also, my rhythm sucks.

We are close to the Romanian team and every time I look up, I catch Angelika's smile. I see her bend her back like she has no skeleton and is made of liquid matter, so perfect and so light. She seems to be doing it on purpose, a master class in effortless grace and control, because it isn't normal to be so smiley during training. Or maybe she's playing to a hidden camera, the prodigy, always on top of her game, always strong and sure of herself. Protected from pain and from breaking. And maybe that's true, for her. Bodies have gifts, it's how you're born: some can sing and some have the best brain for maths and can explain x and y factors as if they were nothing. In our case it's not only about training. Champions are champions right from the start. There are no miracles, there never will be. Anna, Benedetta, and I, for example, we are diligent, we work hard and have managed to become decent gymnasts. But none of us will ever be a star. We are good enough to be useful to the team, to help our stars and to pass the ball to those whose names will be remembered. I am proud of this too but it's clearly not enough. And seeing Angelika's inbuilt genius, wanting to be her and wanting to beat her, it's clearly not enough to be able to get to the individual apparatus finals or to the All Around on Sunday.

Let alone to the Olympics.

On the uneven bars, Carla lights up the whole hall with a *Nabieva*. I watch her shadow on the wall, like that of a superhero, the lines of her body showing the world she can fly and that even in this universe, magic exists and sometimes it is so visible and so near. Her outline is perfect, the neatness of her sequence is extraordinary. She's fast. She has control. Her gymnastics is a poem about love. As soon as she lands, with the full twisting double tuck she has been doing so well for a year that she is almost bored with it, she winks at Nadia and makes a rude gesture towards Angelika, who isn't even looking.

'Now you're afraid, aren't you, doggie?' she hisses.

A hand clutching at her chest, she also pretends to be Coach Florin, Angelika's hero, having his ultra-famous heart attack.

Rachele's eyes are darting from side to side, checking out if the other coaches are staring at her little prodigy. During the competition she's not allowed to look at the jury's reaction, but today she can enjoy the moment. Have they seen what Carla can do at the bars? I don't think they have and I feel sorry for Rachele because maybe they will all stare now, when it's my turn and they'll see me struggle. They'll see I am made of hard wood and fragile clay. Of fear and pain.

I jump, grab the lower bar, and hear Rachele shouting out my usual mistakes, calling me lazy, while my body loses confidence, then precision. I'm not doing well and we all know it, but for every one of her words, I do even worse. More than that, I fulfil her prophecy. I become lazy. The loser. My gymnastics is a bad song that hurts your ears and annoys you. When I dismount, trying to keep my chest up, Alex says, 'OK,' and nobody adds anything. Rachele's silence is worse than her insults.

I tie my hair bun twice and wait for my heart to slow down. I've been waiting for years now.

When it's Nadia's turn, everything stops. Her eyes, her feet, Rachele's breathing. The million snowflakes in the huge sky above the Cozia Forest take a break too, hanging in mid-air.

'What's the matter?' Carla asks her.

'Nothing.'

But we all know what the matter is. Nadia is seeing things. Once I heard her explain that she saw things as if they'd been filmed at low resolution. As if instead of coming to life through her eyes, they come through a very old cell phone.

'Or downloaded from a very slow internet connection,' she'd told us.

This makes it even scarier for her. She doesn't recognize the images as her own or chosen by her. Like if someone is sending them to her. But from where? And why?

I start counting to a hundred. The Polish boys start sniggering. Karl is looking. And some of the other coaches are looking at us at last.

'Nadia, go on, it's your turn.'

'One second.'

'Nadia, you're scaring everybody,' Rachele says. 'Get a grip.'

I can sense Nadia's jaw clenching so hard it could break her teeth.

'OK, OK. I'm right here.'

But Nadia isn't right here. She is somewhere there, and she can't go anywhere and she can't do anything. When she gets stuck like this, Carla will often go up to her and call her an idiot or tell her to 'Move, for fuck's sake. Now!' Sometimes she pinches Nadia's bottom, to try and make her understand she should deal with it as if it were a joke. A pinch on the bottom. Just one of those things in life that you take, like Alex's fingers moving up and down and left and right inside you from the age of 10 onwards, or the Bible to be read ten times a day by the voice of your godly mother.

No need to turn it into a big drama or be too precious about it.

So this time Carla goes up to her and we watch the usual sequence of her cold looks and her encouraging whispers. But Nadia does not react and all I can think is that she is pretty even when she's crazy and even when she's paralysed. Her hair catches the light and looks so shiny, so beautiful. She is as still as a picture I'd stare at for hours if it were on my bedside table. I'd look closely at it to understand how hips can be so delicate and how it's possible that a girl's skin can glow as if it were made of tiny pink lights.

'Listen, little snail. Move,' Carla says.

But Nadia remains frozen.

'Do you want me to bite you?' Carla says. 'What is it you can see inside that weird head of yours? Tragedies and broken necks? Are you dreaming that pathetic Angelika over there will do us a favour and shatter a foot? Die?'

Nadia doesn't even look at her. Carla seems to be doubting her abracadabra will work and even though she keeps giving Nadia orders, you can see by the way her neck is tilted and her hands are moving that something isn't right. Then, as though her freeze-up had never happened, Nadia smiles.

'Here I am.'

And here she is and here she goes. She arches her back a couple of times, runs to the bars, begins her routine, gets the *Maloney* wrong halfway through, starts again and does it beautifully. Her wall shadow is shorter than

Carla's. And lacks definition. She'll never manage to perform a straight full twist followed by a *Derwael-Fenton*, but she's still our second best. And she is still a very strong gymnast. She does well in spite of the error and, as usual, in spite of her fears, which are very often also our fears. And so we breathe out – jolly, relieved – and we smile at Nadia's swerve from danger, at our swerve from danger. We hope it won't happen during the competition, but hey.

Here she is. Here we are.

Not one of us is here against her will. Our families don't force us. It's not as if we're footballers and they're getting rich exploiting us. And it's not as if our parents can really look after us – or protect us – when we spend so much time away from them. Except for Caterina, of course. Her mother did rescue her. But, as Nadia says, statistically, there's already been one: a mum has taken her daughter away and the fractures that have been healed have already been hers.

We are here to stay.

When we were 7 or 9 years old, we complained. To the young assistant coaches, who seemed nice enough. And to our parents. We tried again at 10. 11. We sometimes told them what was going on, the pills to block our pain or to calm our panic. We repeated the names we were called day in day out. Those who managed to at 13 said something about Alex. We said, 'I don't like it, Mum.' Or 'Is that OK, Coach?' Or 'Can you stop him?' But, when nothing changed, we started complaining less, until we were silent.

Until we smiled again. And again we bowed.

Now, when we talk of other gymnasts, of our rivals, we use the same names that hurt us so much. Now these are our words and when we say them we feel nothing. They mean nothing. Gymnastics is all of our lives. This team is all of our lives. Each one of us has her own secret plan, a reason to stay.

I like to think that if I'm good enough and make it to the Olympics, I'll gain money. With money, I'll be able to get a bigger house for my family and one day buy a gym where I will teach and host local and regional championships which will bring in even more money. We will work together at the gym, the three of us. Me, Mum, and Dad. Maybe I'll marry someone nice – not a gymnast, a coach or an athlete, for sure – and I might have a couple of kids who won't be as poor as I am. This alone will make me a better person and make my life better too. My gym will be painted in shades of purple. Or blue. Yes, blue. There will be a sauna and huge windows facing out onto a garden. And when I'm done with this life, the one I have now, I will not put on weight. I'll jog and swim. I'll laugh. And talk.

'Time to go and eat,' says Rachele.

'To go and fast!' hisses Carla.

Nadia grabs Carla's hand and leads her towards the exit. We follow, glancing back as Angelika executes a spectacular floor exercise. Double layout full, *Mukhina*. *Silivas*. The sequence of her elements, of her routine, is the most difficult I've ever seen in this arena. Or maybe ever. Her gymnastics is beauty itself. And magic itself. Then, as if we haven't just witnessed her supernatural powers, we busy ourselves and Carla imitates the way ducks, lions, and cats walk, going up on her tiptoes, trying to make the whole team laugh. And we do laugh when she pretends she's a snake on the floor. Bums sticking up and tongues hissing, we copy her, bent double, trying to rid ourselves of Angelika's existence, sequence, and beauty. Nadia also waves at Karl from the floor and Carla says, 'Stop it, you idiot.' But she's laughing and anyway Karl hasn't seen us: his eyes are still on Angelika, her perfect body, her perfect routine and maybe he too, just like me, is thinking *At night Angelika is a cat.*

And maybe, at night, Angelika is safe.

It quickly turns to evening, like in the movies when the sky and the clouds change colour in five seconds and life goes into fast forward and suddenly we are in front of Rachele's bathroom for our post-exercise ice bath. No matter how much I know it's good for me, it's hard to get into the tub. At first it really hurts and I only want to run away. But after exactly sixty seconds, one minute to count down through gritted teeth, the pleasure floods in. I feel it in my throat at first, then the warmth spreads everywhere, to my bum, my eyes, to the root of each hair. I shout out in ecstasy and I don't care if Rachele or anyone hears me. My skin tingles, and twitches, my muscles shiver and quiver and I can feel them thanking me.

'Thank you, Martina,' they say. 'Thank you for having the courage to immerse yourself today, for feeling your heart stop and then beat again. You truly are a warrior.'

We warriors then all go and have our physio session with Alex and we are almost allowed to relax during it – let our muscles get the best out of his practice – as he never touches us under our leotards when we are away for a championship.

'He might be scared of the police in foreign countries,' Carla sometimes says, brushing us off. 'Or he might become a different monster in different time zones. Maybe here he eats people.'

And she might laugh too.

But I can never bring myself to join in with her laughter. I don't even think it's laughter, it just sounds like it. I just think Carla has chosen not to care. But she does care. She pretends she is not hurt but she is hurt. Just like Nadia, who in order to survive, has chosen to move the fear from Alex to that of everything. I guess I have chosen to repeat things in sequence. And stay as silent as I can.

During today's session I stay as silent as I can too. He does not touch me inside and I count until I zone out. Until I see my body as still as a corpse. Then as stone. I try to breathe in the smell of the massage bed – the plastic, the soap to clean it. I try not to get infected with the smell of his body. I try to imagine the supermarket where the soap was purchased. Paid for. Here are the four euros, thank you, have a lovely day.

'Send Carla in,' he says.

And I send Carla in.

Back in our room, wrapped in my bathrobe, I lie on my bed, my skin red with ice and heat, and I call home. Not that I want to, but I made a promise and it's better to keep that promise when the other two are still out. As the phone rings, I picture the girls eyeing up Karl and the other good-looking boys, all the Spanish ones, or the French one they admire for his 'juicy French butt'. I picture Carla and Nadia, identical but with different colour hair, like twins in a horror movie. I also picture them playing some kind of trick on Angelika, like cutting through her leotard or staining it with ketchup or something disgusting like spit or cat pee. I hate myself for spending so much time thinking about them. I'd really like to be able to stop doing it.

But then again, it's just another one to add to the list of things I'd like to be able to stop doing.

When Dad answers the phone, he immediately tells me that according to a celebrity monk's almanac of prophecies, tomorrow and Sunday are my lucky days.

'It's most likely you'll qualify and it's more likely than not that I will find a new job. Very soon, maybe even as soon as tomorrow,' he says. 'Next week if I have to stretch it.'

'Awesome,' I say.

'Maybe the factory is reopening as we speak and everyone will be taken back on. Your luck is also my luck!' His voice is a slur and I can hear the drink in it. 'You will win and you will fall and you will win again. In love, in life, in everything,' he continues. 'My mousy mouse, you must be happy!'

'Where's Mum?'

'She went to clean the salon. To pick up hair,' he says. 'She dreams of finding it in her mouth and wakes up trying to pull it out from between her teeth. Cute. And weird. I suppose this is one of the reasons we, the Family of Mice, love her, isn't it?'

He starts laughing and I say, 'Yes, we do love her.'

I say it even though saying 'love' or any phrase with the word love in it makes me feel sad. I mimic a couple of kissing noises and put the phone down. As soon as I hear the click, I start crying.

At least this time he didn't sing 'That's Amore'.

I look out of the window, to see if the wolves are there in the whitest white. Instead, I see Nadia and Carla, and a few Romanian girls, some Chinese gymnasts and some

I don't know where from. They look like they're friends, sharing jokes and laughs, but are probably saying mean things to each other in their own languages. I open the window and the cold air hits me, together with the sound of the girls' voices.

From here it's like hearing howls.

During tournaments, when we aren't training, we often challenge each other, to see who can hold a handstand the longest or somersault through the air. Tonight, close to the dark forest, they are competing for who can stand the longest with their hands in the snow. From up in my room, I feel their pain, freezing fingers, blood becoming ice. It's almost cool to watch these Olympic hopefuls challenging each other out there, ten degrees below zero as I stand in the warm, my blood pumping after the ice bath and the heating full on.

I've never taken part in these kinds of competitions, but later, at home, I always try out whatever the challenge was, timing myself, just to see how I would do if the opportunity to compete came up.

I'd do good.

Now, as they endure freezing handstands in the snow, I watch their upside-down backs exposed, the snow still falling and Nadia winning against Angelika and Carla. When she finally comes down, everyone applauds her. I clap too, and wonder if the other two – the champions, the strongest of us all – lost on purpose. Whether Carla and Angelika are both way too clever to risk hurting themselves just before the team qualification. And whether they are both way too clever not to know that they are both using Nadia, while also making her weaker.

WEDNESDAY

'This is the first time I've fancied someone so much,' Nadia is saying, as I wake up.

I'm cold. It's still dark. I think I am still me but I need to check the red hair and all.

'Even if he's short?' Carla laughs. 'Even if he's not me?'

I can count my heartbeats without needing to hold a finger to my wrist. All I have to do is listen to what's going on inside. My body is an empty room in which the beating of my heart is loud, making space for itself in the gaps between my flesh, my organs, the blood. My heart is the size of a fist, then if I want it gets bigger, like a ball, the sun. I can see my blood go in and out of the ventricles of this sun, round my veins, my capillaries. I'd love to say it out loud, to tell Carla and Nadia, 'Can you see how my blood gives colour to my lips? Can you see that if I concentrate I can warm up my hands and make my heart the size of the sun?'

But because I am still me even in Romania, I am still the silent one even in Romania. So it's Nadia who speaks instead.

'I bumped into him in the downstairs loo last night,' she says. 'I was jumping up and down to feel the soda bubbles in my tummy. He came in and he laughed.'

'When did you go there?' asks Carla. 'What was I doing?'

'You were talking to Anna and Benedetta,' says Nadia. 'Obsessing about the imaginary fat girl.'

'Anna has such greasy hair. I don't understand it. With all that money, why doesn't she buy herself the most expensive conditioner? And shampoo. And hairdresser.'

Blah blah blah. How many times have I heard her say things about Anna's hair or Anna's money? My sun-heart skips a beat. It would be best to make it small again, from the size of a whole hot plasma mega star, to that of a fist.

'He smiled at me,' says Nadia. 'Then we said *hi* at the same time.'

'How romantic,' says Carla, her voice like glass.

'He did a cartwheel in the corridor and I copied him. I also did a backflip and he copied me. We carried on with different moves until we found ourselves face to face, my tummy against his tummy, my handstand resting against his—'

'His penis?'

'His handstand!'

I can feel the sensation Nadia had in her back in that moment. How her ponytail jolted when she was in the bridge position and what the world looked like from there. Upside down, of course. And wonky, like from inside a pool. To feel this way is the special magic of the bridge position, like the special magic of a double somersault is to hold your breath and turn into a flying fish. But I say nothing about blood and red lips, pools and flying fishes.

'We touched noses, too. We rubbed them upside down,' Nadia continues.

'Gross!' says Carla. 'Not sexy at all.'

'It was so nice,' says Nadia, and starts laughing. 'I think noses can be very sexy.'

Carla climbs on top of her and forces her to rub their noses together and I force myself not to look and start my counting. I get to seven hundred, then fall asleep.

The next thing I hear is Carla.

'I hate that bitch,' she is saying, and I know she's talking about Angelika.

I hear their duvet moving, then footsteps on the carpet. I open my eyes and Nadia and Carla are looking through the window. Nadia is completely naked and all Carla has on is a fluorescent bandage around her left knee which glows in the moonlight, like those little star stickers on bedroom walls. Those same star stickers that eventually stop glowing and leave black glue on the walls forever.

Seen from behind they look like little boys, their bottoms round and firm, their legs short, their backs arched. Two little boys of maybe 5 or 7 years old, with long hair and bruises and scratches all over their skin. This too would be a lovely picture, the whiteness outside and the blonde and the brunette staring outside, lit only by the sky, their hands grabbing each other, confirming their eternal pact of togetherness, as they curse Angelika. Angelika the mad, Angelika the enemy, Angelika the dog that needs to die.

'But why are you still running? Florin is dead, you idiot!' Carla shouts out of the open window.

'You can stop now!' Nadia yells. 'We got the sense of it, you are a show-off!'

They hold on tighter to each other, shaking their heads, and they hop on the spot before rushing back under the duvet. They are still giggling at the cold as I shut my eyes again. I can feel the ice on their skin and as I cross back into my dreams I can see Carla and Nadia's naked bodies, mixed up with the hair in my mum's mouth and Angelika on all fours like a dog and I can hear the rhythm of Nadia Comaneci's most famous sequence on the uneven bars. It's a solfeggio I know by heart. I wonder if I can force my heartbeat to copy that rhythm too.

I'm still dreaming when the second alarm goes off. I stretch, pop a painkiller, then get in the bathroom so I can rinse off my dreams and check the level of redness of my hair. I like being underwater. I can hold my breath under the jet for a very long time. If I hadn't chosen gymnastics, swimming would have suited me well and maybe once I'm finished with hand holds, it still could be an option. Maybe I'll swim to the competitions.

I'll cross all oceans and all of the immense seas.

Back in the bedroom, we are focused and tense. We pull on our blue leotards for the team qualifications, covering our bodies from the crotch to the shoulders. We spray some glue to stick the fabric to our bums so it won't move. We can get deductions if we fix our leotards during a routine or if any of our underwear is showing. These leotards are not as fancy as the one I'll wear on Sunday if I get through, and that's why I prefer them. I always like those for the qualifications better – they're simple, only one colour and not too flashy. The ones for the All

Around finals are bright pink and covered in way too many sequins.

I don't like pink and I don't like sequins. I am not even sure I like finals.

Nadia and Carla fix each other's nail polish, smooth each other's hair buns, and check how they look from behind. They look amazing, they agree. They turn me around to check how I look. My thighs. My butt. *Your body is not yours, it's the team's,* I hear Rachele say.

'Aren't you worried you'll get cellulite?' Carla asks me. I'm guessing I don't look amazing from behind.

'Did you know redheads get cellulite early? Are you scared?' Nadia says.

'No,' I say. Even though the real answer is yes. Now I *am* scared of cellulite. I hate cellulite and cellulite has to stay away from me. Just like carbs, Rachele's squeaky voice, Alex's fast breathing, and the wolves out there.

Nadia pulls the elastic wraps on Carla's knee as tight as they will go and sticks on the knee support. Carla sighs.

'Does it hurt?' Nadia asks.

'What do you think? Two lots of surgery, it'll hurt forever,' Carla replies.

'Yes, but today, how badly?'

'Stop bugging me and pull tighter.'

'I'm pulling, but you've got to tell Alex and Rachele if it hurts.'

'Listen, headcase, do I have to kick you in the butt or something? The knee is fine. I can do pain no problem. What I can't do is your voice.'

I slip on my wartime iPod, choose shuffle mode, and carry on getting ready while I secretly watch them. Have we taken enough care of that left knee? I am starting to feel the pain it might cause each one of us. It's the same with guilt or responsibility, we share it. And because we share it, we will all be weak on Sunday too, when we need Carla to be strong and to win her medals. One body, one heart. One knee.

In the canteen all the teams are quiet and orderly, each at their own table, each with their coach and physios at the head of the table, everyone wearing their club's track-suit. I am sure many of them have an Alex. Quiet and kind from the outside, all formal and sleazy when needed, but capable of the worst behind closed doors. Have the other gymnasts asked for help and nobody's heard them either? And did they feel that saying it out loud was so painful it seemed their teeth could fall out and their heart would break? Did their coach, just like Rachele, promise them they were now safe?

Are we all counting to a thousand then to a million, at night?

The girls have too much make-up on and the boys have too much gel in their hair. Today eight of the sixteen teams will be eliminated. We shouldn't worry and we kind of know already who will be gone – that Irish team, the Greek one for sure, and so on. Yet we do worry, also because not being worried means not being humble. Or good. And it's also bad luck.

We drink our coffee, eat our cardboard half biscuits, and listen to Rachele. This morning we pay more attention mostly because we're frightened of what lies ahead. We even manage to listen to Alex without hatred spilling out of us, or feeling faint, as he tells us to warm up properly and how to take care of our injuries. Nadia is beginning to go pale, Anna looks panicky, Benedetta is shaking, Carla is being louder than usual as she psychs herself up at Rachele's dos and don'ts.

'And don't eat too much,' Rachele finishes, looking at our plates.

'As if,' Carla says.

I immediately decide to leave half of the half biscuit.

'When we get to the gym, as Alex just said, we do our warm-ups. The qualifiers start at eleven,' Rachele says. 'Carla, please stop giggling. And, Nadia, please, don't encourage her. Respect, elegance, honesty. I don't want to hear any comments on the opposing teams. Be strong, because you are strong. Be brave, because you are brave. That's why you are here and all the other girls that started gymnastics with you have disappeared.'

She looks at us. Is she secretly selecting who will soon disappear from this club too? Me?

'Benedetta,' she snaps. 'Redo your hair. We are one heart. One body. And with hair like that our body sucks. Right. Let's get to work. Be good, girls.'

Work, work, work. Rachele says it so often, just listening to her repeating the word work is work. The same way she's always repeating, 'Be strong because you are strong' and that we have to be good girls. We know her catchphrases by heart but before a competition we need to hear them again and again and again. Because what she says is always important in terms of spells and superstition and repetition and because she's been the most constant presence in our lives so – despite everything – we have to stick to her and to what we imagine is also a nuance of love. It's not like we have a choice anyway. We have spent more hours with Rachele than with our mothers. She knows about the holes in our teeth, our braces, our blood tests. She knows our past, our present. She probably knows our future too, what we will become and who will really get into the national team. She knows who has not fulfilled their promise and in spite of all efforts, is getting worse. She probably also knows whether or not I'll qualify in the first fifteen on Sunday. And who, sooner or later, will surrender to the horror. She knows, for sure, every single detail of what Alex has done to me. And to us.

'Leave it with me,' she said. 'You're safe now, Marti.'

It had taken all my courage from this and all the other universes, to put one word after the other. To say them out loud. It had taken me nights of crying and vomiting to be able to look her in the eye and to tell her that during most physio sessions Alex would stick his fingers inside me. That sometimes, I wasn't even sure I had breasts when he began doing it, he reached for them and gave me massages. And that I could often hear him panting while he was working on me, touching me, caressing me. Is it rape, Coach? Can you make him stop, please?

'Don't worry,' she said. 'Let me look into that. And thank you for trusting me.'

She hugged me.

For about two and a half hours I believed her. I believed the strength of her hug. I thought that by summoning up all my courage, I had been the pioneer I am supposed to be, and I had fixed it. I could see myself watching Alex being dragged away by the police, never seeing him again and finding out on the news that he was in prison. I imagined writing to the wife. Then erasing the words on the card. Then writing them again.

But when the time of my next physio session came, all was the same as ever. In the room there was Alex. No Rachele. And for sure no police. He was in a good mood. His voice was gentle.

'Now, Marti,' he said, 'what you have been saying to Rachele sounds terrifying. And I am so sorry you had to be afraid for no reason. You've completely mistaken my practice and yes, perhaps I'm the one to blame for that. I am sure I am: who's the adult here, right? Point is, I didn't give you the key information for you to understand that all I do is for a medical reason. Watch this.'

He showed me a low-fi video of a chiropractor doing something to someone's hips. As I was watching the clip, I zoned out and started counting, so I didn't pass out. When the clip was finished, I lay down on my belly as he began working my hips. I had reached number 1,007 when his medical finger was medically back inside me. And half an hour later, having reached number 4,023, I was back in the gym.

It was two years ago.

Floor exercise is my speciality. The beam is my weak spot. I can't say if I'm strong enough to make it on Sunday or ever, because it's not easy to be able to see and understand yourself from the inside. It's not easy to understand if you are good when they tell you that you are good. Or if you are safe when they tell you that you are safe. So today all I know is that I'm a redhead, and redheads get cellulite earlier. I know it's better to eat less and to work harder. To smile and to fight for the team. I also know that when Carla prays at night, when she recites the *Our Father*, she's trying to figure everything out too, and that when Nadia spits her food out into a napkin she's doing just the same. I know that's why Benedetta cuts herself near her pelvis, where the leotard will cover her, and that sometimes she manages to do it with her nails but she mostly uses a razor. Looking around at the other tables

I know many of these coaches or assistant coaches insult or assault the girls and the boys in their teams. That's also why loud shuffle music is better than words, being strong is better than being weak, surviving seems better than dying.

Half of half a biscuit will forever be better than nothing.

Carla nudges Nadia and they start watching Karl. Even Karl seems more serious this morning; so much is expected of him and who knows if he's had a good night's sleep. Karl peeks at Nadia and Carla winks at him.

'Stop it, you idiot,' Nadia says. 'Why would you wink at him? He's mine.'

I can see the anger in Nadia's eyes. In the tension of her whole body.

'You're such a pain. And *you* are mine only. I'm going to speak to him by tongue,' Carla says.

I turn round and Carla is licking her lips. Her lips get shiny with saliva while she hides her mouth from the coach behind her hand. But she really wants the rest of us to see her, as well as Karl's whole team. And of course, we all do see her.

'Do it like me,' Carla tells Nadia. 'Let's make him go crazy.'

Nadia is about to copy her but instead stares at Carla's tongue as if she's studying her glossy and luminous saliva.

'I hate you,' she says to Carla.

'You love me.'

She loves her.

On the other side of the canteen, Angelika is looking deadly serious, not even blinking while listening to her coach. In my opinion, to be able to keep yourself from blinking is a sign of utter dedication. I'd like to be Romanian, I think, right here and now. Because the Romanian gymnasts are really beautiful and not at all unhappy and hunched like care workers, who are the only Romanians that get mentioned on TV or by Carla. Not only are they more beautiful, they are also usually better at gymnastics.

My dad is always going on about how in this messed-up world no one can look after their own children. Nannies leave their own kids behind and move to another country to look after the children of slightly better-off mothers, who don't look after their own kids so they can go to work. This, he says, turns into an absurd vicious circle. This, he says, is a sick world.

'Especially if you consider that the super-rich, like famous actresses,' he adds, 'adopt dirt-poor children, who themselves are other parents' children and mothers, and this too must say something about our idea of love, right?'

And usually he then goes on to say that it might be a good thing, a thing that works in some way, and in hundreds, thousands, millions of years we'll have created a system with a fluidity of its own, mega families of very faraway mothers that mother other mothers' children because it might even be better.

'It might even be better not to just mingle with your own blood. It might be a stepup in terms of civilization, and bring in peace. Like giraffes having long necks and some people not being scared of blood so they can be doctors while others can't. Maybe our way of developing a long neck is not taking care of our own kids anymore: imagine what would happen if that was the world system, imagine how racism would vanish? The idea of owning a land, a country? Wars would end!' he says, and at that point he always adds, 'But for now, mousy, we're still here, and it mostly has to do with money, so we've been really lucky in this respect too, because we couldn't even afford help, so we brought you up ourselves one hundred per cent. Of course, with the help of Gymnastics.'

Of course with the help of Gymnastics.

I slept in the offices that had to be cleaned, and I was never apart from my parents. But when I took up gymnastics, order took over too, other adults began watching over me, helped bring me up. There were the coaches. The doctors. And even if some of them were like Alex, others really cared about me. There was the team now, and my life outside our home and our family. There was the opportunity to better my life, whatever that really means, and to make a home out of a gym.

I have always liked the idea that in taking up gymnastics, I relieved Mum and Dad of myself. The club pays for all my travelling and food when I'm away at competitions or anywhere with them, plus they sometimes help if I need a new leotard or something we can't afford but really need. The club pays for my school books, my physiotherapy, my pills, and a part of me is so proud of this it makes it a secret driving force for not stopping.

I want to be good, so I am good.

Another plus is that when I'm away, my parents sleep in my bedroom, so they have a room to themselves and don't have to crash on the couch. Sometimes I wonder what they say to each other when I'm not around. Maybe they make plans. Or lists of the dreams that might seem more reachable when I'm not there.

That's why they probably didn't listen to me about Alex either.

We leave the canteen, in a line of well-behaved girls. We really are very small, very short, and I notice it even more when I walk past the waiters or I am near some other hotel guests who must think we look like aliens. It's humiliating to see the world from down here, the level of most people's bellybuttons. It's humiliating yet fascinating, just like many other things in life. Starving so you can be called beautiful. Staying silent so you can be called strong. Lowering your eyes so you can be called humble and grateful and graceful.

We are finally free when we cross the white field and it's us alone. Us, the gymnasts. Us, the good girls. No one is commanding us. No one is calling us names. And now we really are striking, and now we really are an army. We cross the bridge intoxicated with the cold, as we leave the forest and the wolves behind. As we leave all of our thoughts behind.

We just walk, and run. We laugh.

The arena is all lit up. The audience is here, the seats almost full. We acknowledge them but try not to get distracted by them. I feel their gaze. I hear their sounds, their shoes on the floor, the spatters of applause, the rumble of their chatter. I feel their excitement, which becomes my excitement. Angelika's name shouted out. That of Carla. I hear their heartbeats. Then, mine.

I synchronize them all.

To try to gather more strength and focus, I keep some distance from my teammates while they take off their tracksuits. They remain in their leotards while I am still zipped up, like I'm inside a cage. I can see Carla and Nadia repeating their stupid rhyme and I lip-read the words about the blue pooh. The jury is assembling and the scoreboards are lighting up. I concentrate on the brown outline drawn with lip pencil around Rachele's mouth and on the orangey lipstick she has filled it with. She's used too much again and the result is doughy, like Plasticine. She'll have lipstick stains on one or two of her teeth and when I see them I know I will lose some more trust in her, for failing to be careful enough to check her teeth. So I stop looking, because I'd rather not know. Same reason I will never tell her about Alex again. I'd rather not hear her lies again. And never crumble again in the silence that would follow.

'I need you to keep an eye on Carla and Nadia,' Rachele whispers to me. 'Those two make each other strong but they can also make each other very weak and you are well aware of how we must look out for each other and we all must especially look out for Carla. Right?'

'Right,' I say.

Or maybe I don't. We both don't care if I did.

'Please,' she continues, 'if there's anything wrong, come and tell me. If you see them do something, I don't know, dangerous, or that looks dangerous to you, come and tell me.'

'Dangerous? Like what?'

Like flying backwards three times in the air trying not to die? Like being left alone with Alex since you were 10? Like not eating or bingeing on pills? Like what?

'I'm not asking you to be a snitch,' Rachele says. 'I'm asking you to help me keep an eye on their, let's say, peace of mind. Because *their* peace of mind is what?'

'*My* peace of mind?'

'Exactly! And now back to you, Marti. Take care of the *Tsukahara*. With hard work you can achieve anything, my love. Remember to smile, especially when an exercise goes well. You can be pretty too, you know? Be the pioneer of your future.'

I want to throw up. *My love? You can be pretty too?* I feel beyond doubt the ugliest girl in the team. Or in this hemisphere. On top of that I am also the invisible one, the best behaved one, made to share with the two prettiest and strongest girls in the team just so I can snitch on them. If this was a movie, I'd have braces and glasses and spots on my skin.

I clench my jaw and feel it creaking all the way to my eyes. I clench more and try to feel it in the skull too. Why talk to me now, right before the competition? Rachele ought to get a different job and get as far away as possible. I feel exhausted, lost, until I get my breath back and it's in that second that there is a thud and then one vast whispered murmuring.

The stillness that follows is the stillness of disaster. We know something bad has happened even before checking with our eyes. We've been raised by these very loud and terrible thuds followed by stillness.

It's our soundtrack.

As the world starts moving again, I watch the doctors run towards the mat and paramedics running with a stretcher. I bend down to see who is lying on it, on the mat under the bars, because a thud is always the sound a body makes when slamming on the floor, and a murmur is always the crowd's murmur when a body remains motionless. All I can see are a pair of small legs and feet, completely still. Feet pointing straight up to the ceiling without moving, not trembling, nothing. Seeing unmoving feet, not even trembling and without being able to see a face, is worse than seeing the whole body not moving in one go. My teammates have their hands in front of their mouths. Some are terrified, others look like they are almost laughing. It must be the nerves.

Rachele tells us to sit down and be still and quiet and so we do. Toy soldiers, good girls, we sit still and quiet.

'What a disaster,' Nadia says.

'You don't know what happened,' Carla replies. 'Maybe

it's Angelika. Let me see if the dragonfly got herself squashed.'

'Don't joke.'

'Don't you want me to be happy, Nadia?'

Nadia looks at Carla. I think she is picturing Angelika lifeless on the mat, or out of action, maybe paralysed. We've seen that happen already, it wouldn't be the first time and won't be the last either. Maybe Nadia is already seeing this sequence uploaded onto YouTube. Clicked on a thousand times, commented on and voted for. Thumbs up. Thumbs down.

Nadia starts breathing so heavily I think she'll faint.

Carla takes Nadia's hand and strokes it. She strokes the back of her hand then turns it over and strokes the palm too. I guess she wants her to feel two different sorts of caresses. Then she pouts and rests her head on Nadia's shoulder, and looks so sweet as she whispers how a dead or damaged Angelika would be an option not to be scoffed at. Carla's hair is tied up in a bun as yellow as honey. She has blue eyeshadow on her eyelids, and her tiny, manicured hands are still stroking Nadia while she repeats the words 'coma' and 'paralysis' and says, 'Out of the games, out of my life.'

Nadia is pale. Like an actress in a costume drama, the protagonist of a romantic tale set in the eighteenth century or perhaps the seventeenth, who coughs all the way through the second half, precisely to let us know that she's going to die. Which of course she does at the end, of TB or consumption.

'You're shaking,' says Carla.

'I'm not,' she replies. 'I'm fine.'

'Let's talk about Karl,' says Carla. 'How we'll kiss him to make him forget he's so short.'

'Please,' hisses Nadia. 'Leave me alone.'

The crowd moves away, the stretcher is carried out and on it, like a limp rag, is a tiny Polish gymnast. I don't remember seeing her before. Now I will see her in my dreams forever.

The adults are still talking to each other as they move away and the girl is carried out in a neck brace. No one will tell us anything, at least until the end of the day. So I take off my tracksuit and I start warming up. I know it's what we are supposed to do. Work. And deep inside, we are all actually relieved, because as Nadia has taught us, the statistics of potential disaster are now on our side. One of the girls has got hurt already, a stretcher has been carried through the gym and this has immediately made us safer.

But with this relief, comes guilt.

'Sad, but nothing we can do about it,' Rachele says. 'Let's get to work.'

'Don't worry, girls,' Alex says. And the 's' of girls in my mind becomes a slippery slimy snake. I kill it with a stick. Cook it. Eat it.

The jury takes its position. Rachele tells us the usual million things and gives us the running order of competition. I almost check out her teeth, the lipstick smear, but I manage not to look. Nadia is the first in line and we say, 'Break a leg,' and saying it I think about our broken legs, and suddenly the wolves in the forest appear again in my mind. Could I learn how to live with them out there? Would they protect me and kill for me? I imagine the cave I'd keep warm in, a bonfire, sleeping peacefully near the animals. I know they are good with game hunting as a team and I can do game hunting as a team too.

'Be a good girl,' Rachele says to Nadia. 'Be strong.'

'I want you naked in the middle of the arena, if you make it to the first ten at the All Around,' Carla whispers.

'Shut up, you idiot.'

But I know Carla helps her when she does this, because Nadia gets distracted and she can rest her mind from her demons and monsters. And in fact from that moment on, we become the army and the game hunters that we can be.

Carla's words work better than Rachele's. So does her talent.

When she runs towards any jump, it's like we were running with her. We follow her beauty and fast pace on the uneven bars and we celebrate her perfection on the balance beam. By the time we move to the floor exercise, thanks to her energy that becomes our energy, we are all doing great. We are focused. We are a team. Despite Benedetta's general weakness and Anna's average performance, we are getting near a 160 score that will put us in the first ten teams. I do OK on the beam, Carla is a star throughout, and Nadia is strong and confident when she begins her last routine on the floor. After her wolf turn double, the twisting split leap and a beautiful front tuck, she salutes the jury, proud of all the beauty and the precision she's capable of. Her back bends as she waves, her humble smile lights the entire arena. The audience responds with a booming applause. Carla nods in acknowledgement.

'I love you,' she tells Nadia.

'I love you too,' Nadia replies.

It's my turn on the floor and I have to touch my nose several times before my routine, but no one notices. As the music begins, the memory of the muscles reacts before that of the mind. I start with an acrobatic sequence and I'm quick in the jumps, in the runs, and my shape is tight. I squeeze my bum, tuck my tummy in. I land perfectly on my third diagonal. My rebound is clean, and so are my combination passes, as I continue with a double layout followed by a tuck landing.

Maybe Romania has really turned me into a winner, I think.

On my last diagonal I also dare to think about the team's reaction as they witness my effortless grace and that's exactly the moment in which I lose control, and all of my elegance. I go for the front flip, a shaky roundoff then a triple twist, before losing my body shape. After I punch, and twist once more, I land with my feet apart and make two extra steps.

I salute the jury and quickly meet Rachele's eyes. Her smile is not quite there. I don't check to see whether Alex is smiling or not.

We move to the vault and Carla is on first. During her magical ninety seconds that last an hour, or maybe an entire lifetime, I am forgotten. They don't need me. And when Carla hypnotizes the arena, time and space expand in her honour and all is forgotten and everyone is forgotten. As she finishes her routine and salutes all the known and unknown universes, I'm sure I see glitter coming from the ceiling.

Trying to grab and welcome some of Carla's magical glitter, I run to the vault, but lose my body shape once again. Maybe her mum is right. Maybe there is a God and Carla is a chosen one.

Nadia, Benedetta, and Anna do their acceptable vaults, then we wait for the sum of our last scores near our bench, drinking water, loosening up our shoulders and legs. Zipping my fleece up and down, I scan in my mind all my mistakes, and start to deduct tenths and hundredths of points from the team's success.

'Fuck, Martina, you were about to ruin us,' Carla says. 'Thank God we didn't need you.'

'Stop,' Nadia tells her. 'We don't do that.'

'Good job, girls,' Rachele says as Carla scores 15.66, Nadia gets a 14.77, and I receive a 13.66. The Useless Ones receive 14, but overall – despite me – the team has done really well and we bring home a solid 168.40. We are in, for sure.

So we smile. And we hug.

We study the scores of the teams that made it to the next phase, and we see the Greeks and the Portuguese girls crying. We've been those girls. We take in the success of the Romanians and the Chinese, and try to digest it. We've been those girls too. We acknowledge the average scores of the Spanish club and move on with life.

'Tonight you can eat carbs,' Rachele tells us. 'You deserve it.'

'You did great,' Alex says.

As usual we try to cancel his voice from the spectrum of the sounds of the world, like those of bombs or cars when crashing, while he goes on and on, commenting on every single second of today's qualifications.

'Why doesn't he shut up?' I hear Nadia say. 'Like forever.'

I turn around and look at her. It's the first time I've heard her say something out loud about Alex in front of the team. It's scarier than I thought.

When we leave the gym at seven, the snow has fallen in mountains around the war-hotel car park. I look at the sky and the snowflakes fill my eyes. They become icy-cold tears, crystals instead of drops, so when no one is looking I stretch my tongue out, waiting for the tickling and the minuscule, magical cold.

Thank God we didn't need you, I hear in my head again.

They all run, shouting out loud, feeling the snow crumble as their boots sink into the white. But I am about to cry and they all notice.

'One body, one heart, Martina!' Carla says. 'You'll be great tomorrow, sorry about earlier. I love you girls.'

And when she says it we know we all need to hug. It's the rule. If Carla makes peace, you make peace. So we do it, we hug and become one body again, squeezed, cheeks against cheeks, arms holding arms, near the vast dark forest.

'Say it.'

'Tomorrow I'll be great,' I say. And I jam my nails hard into my palms.

Tomorrow I'll be great, and tonight we are allowed not only to eat carbs but also to leave the hotel as a treat, to see a world without carpeted halls or score-boards, to think less of falls and broken legs – of how the Polish girl's life might change forever today – and more of what girls our age usually think. I'm not entirely sure what that would be, but it seems to involve being at a shopping mall. It's the best night out we've been offered in months. I would actually say in years, if it didn't sound too pathetic.

We wash, dress up, and plaster too much make-up on. We sit in the minibus and drive to the village. We leave behind the mountains, the river, a closed aqua park, the sound of the wind when it hits the woods. The city centre is clean and I think medieval kind of old. Or maybe some other era, I don't know. Trams pass close by and make the same noise as the ones we have at home. Some of the streets in the outskirts are really wide, the constructions bleak and repetitive, I love this repetition and I love pressing my forehead against the cold bus glass, loud music in my ears, the other girls shut out of my mind. I measure the buildings, study each one of them and compare the colour of the Romanian streetlights with the ones I see after training when I get on the bus back home.

I look at their stars. Their moon.

When I grow up, I could travel and do nothing else. I'd need to work out how to earn money and maybe this idea is better than the gym one. I don't really want children or a husband. Or to work with Mum. I'd far rather hold my forehead against cold car windows in cities I don't know. Study their buildings. Their stars. Their moon. Hear foreign languages, turn them into familiar ones, foreign street corners into familiar ones. I'd rather get lost, disappear, vanish, than always having to be me. And if I have to keep on being me, I'd rather change the backdrop anyway.

'Where are you, my mouse, my love?' Mum would ask on the phone, sounding very far away. And from very far away her squeaks would hurt less.

'I've just arrived in Africa,' I'd say.

'Weren't you in Alaska?'

'I was. Now I'm in Senegal.'

'The snow makes Romania look less revolting,' Carla says, so I cancel her voice more, by turning up the volume more. Also because Romania is in fact striking. Poor, but with music, in striking Romania, I tell myself, is OK. Poor, with no music, back home, is against the law.

Earlier today Carla was interviewed for the *Federation* magazine and posed for the photos, flexing her arm muscles in an imitation of Popeye, like she always does. We stood behind her and smiled. Nadia kissed her and told her that her posture was like a queen's.

'Queen of the dogs, you mean?' Carla said.

'I've had enough of your dogs,' Nadia replied.

'What's with the hair bun?'

'What about it?'

'It's messy. Sweaty. And dirty. Try to be better.'

Nadia had immediately fixed her not-at-all-messy hair and pulled it really tight, trying to be better. While she was pulling it, she had stuck her bottom out, as if by yanking from the top of her head her pelvis got pushed out.

'There, that's more like it. Now you're beautiful as only you can be,' Carla said. 'And anyway, the photographer was a dirty dog. I saw the way he was looking at me. I bet he won't even be able to download the photos because of his sweaty excitement and because he'll be punished, by God, for staring at me like a paedo pig. Did you know that because we are so short, paedos find us more attractive?'

We had looked at her, unable to add anything. She had chosen this way to try to be brave. To try to make it not hurt, and make it a joke. But we know it hurts anyway.

We park in front of the mall and it's exactly like ours. Same brands, same food ads, same neon lights. Same smell of fried chips and frozen vanilla yogurt. I feel at home and, when I realize it, I also feel sad. Rachele tells us we are allowed to split up any way we want, go wherever we want, as long as we met up again 'In precisely one hour and a half under this big M, OK?' We can't help looking up at the big M. Does it remind us all of the word mother? I leave the others, send Mum the Mother a text saying that the first day of competition has gone super well and we are now out for a meal. I write that it's very cold here but I like it, and that I love her.

She calls after one and a half seconds.

'My mousy love, how are you?' she gushes. 'Not too tired? How are you feeling? Are you cold? Don't catch a cold. Are you wearing your hat?'

'I'm good. But I got a 13.10,' I say.

I'm not in the mood to talk to her. I just texted her *I love you*, which I'd never say out loud. And now she is asking me questions, forcing me to hear her voice and her confused words. I let her talk on, worried I'll get snappy like I do at home. Or worse, that she may burst into tears for some minuscule reason, at something I say or don't say. Then I'd feel guilty and we'd be back to square one. I'd be scared of her sadness, which is my sadness too. I'd be aware of my guilt, which again would feed her sadness. Her and Dad's sadness will then eat up all of us, especially me, even though we keep saying we are happy.

It's Wednesday and her hair will already be greasy.

'Who are you sharing a room with, what's the food like, is it cold in the hotel?' she asks, as though she can't stop questioning me.

I don't know which one to answer so I tell her, 'It's all nice.'

She switches to instructions.

'Take care, don't tire yourself out, think of me, don't miss me too much, be happy you are far away from us.'

'I'll see you soon,' I say.

I inhale as much stinky fried-chips air as I can, thinking of when I told them about Alex and they weren't able to save me either. I guess they didn't want to cross the club. And I guess Rachele and Alex's words were more convincing than mine. They might honestly have believed all that medical low-fi crap video. Or maybe they were too weak, just like me. But it's still good that they do get that bed when I'm gone. And that from that bed she can give me instructions on not tiring myself when I'm away.

'OK, I won't tire myself,' I say. 'OK, I'll wear a hat.'

I inhale more, hoping an electromagnetic storm between our house and the Sibiu district will cause the line to die. While I'm counting down the seconds to the end of my patience, I catch a glimpse of Nadia and Carla going into a lingerie shop. I move a few steps closer and spy on them through the windows, while my mum goes on about life and how it is happy but also unhappy, about Dad who still can't find a job but having him home is 'also nice'. Then she rants about the hair on the hairdresser's floor but as usual she adds she shouldn't complain because even if we're not exactly fortunate it's not as if we have to go without shoes.

'We're lucky even when we're unlucky,' I say, repeating another one of their favourite quotes.

'Bravo! Because we love each other.'

'I have to go now, Mum, this is expensive, isn't it? To talk long distance.'

'OK. We're going to have pizza now.'

'Me too, maybe.'

'So we can feel closer,' she says.

It's the saddest sentence ever. All my hunger – which usually is the entire world's hunger so it's really huge – disappears. The remaining little joy that had bubbled up at the idea of being at the mall dissolves. I feel sorry for me. I feel sorry for my parents. Nobody in this world thinks about them, no one needs them. Replaceable in any of their jobs, in all the things they say or do, as humans and as a mother and father. Weak, alone. Deaf.

'So when you are munching on your pizza, make sure you think of us!' she says and I can hear her smile. 'Think about us here in the cosy mousy mouse home.'

Nadia pulls back the dressing room curtain and through the shop window I see her wearing a bra with strawberries on it. She doesn't have any boobs so the cup is empty, like a pocket. She could keep things in that empty space. Stones? Money? Maybe a very small gun. Carla is standing in front of her, chatting and stuffing something into her handbag; she is probably stealing a pair of knickers. It's something blue anyway and seeing her steal is nothing out of the ordinary. Nothing I haven't already seen her do in shops and changing rooms over the last seven years. Once she stole a lamp the size of a watermelon from a gym.

'I threw it in a bin,' she said the day after. That day too she had a gold medal round her neck.

I remember a birthday party at Nadia's house, maybe it was two years ago, when they tried on Nadia's mum's dresses and came out of the bedroom to be admired by us, wearing lace bras and knickers, necklaces, red lipstick smeared on their faces. Carla explained that Nadia's mum had lots of boyfriends and Nadia had laughed and said, 'I met another one of them yesterday.' At the time she had said it in such a funny way that I felt envious of how free and wild her mother was.

'Doesn't it bother you?' Anna had asked.

'Zero bother. I want her to be happy.'

I move away from the shop window and the strawberries on Nadia's bra. I see Benedetta and Anna getting into the pharmacy, then into the make-up shop. I go up all the escalators I can find, take the lift to the eighth floor and again down to the fourth and then the third. I do it ten times. Then, another ten. All I can think is how much I sucked today. And the thud of the Polish girl on the mat.

I don't go into any shops, or into any of the cafés. I let the time pass while forcing myself not to look at clothes, at food or people or anything. I make it my punishment, and my bet. I won't eat, I won't buy, I won't talk. I won't want anything. If I resist, this too will make me stronger. If I resist, I'll do great at the individual qualifications tomorrow. And I'll make it to the All Around on Sunday. If I resist I'll survive all of this pain and I'll be the pioneer of my future.

After two hours of going up and down as the pioneer of my future I'm exhausted and join the team again. They've all bought something, and are holding bubble tea cups. Their mood is great. Or so they are able to show.

'I had a pizza,' I say. Not that anyone asked. But so I am able to show.

On the way back to the parking lot, I listen to Rachele praising us, her good girls, and how today she's so proud. She also says that we are beautiful. By contrast, we are not proud of Rachele, and she is not beautiful, so we don't say anything. Alex, walking near her, looks wasted. We are not too proud of him either.

'All happy, girls?' he asks.

I wonder why his questions have to be so disgusting and pointless. Or exist at all. He's already the silent type, why doesn't he stick to that and decide to completely shut up? A silent monster would be less nauseating than a monster who makes small talk in a Romanian parking lot.

I remember telling him to please stop. I remember his face when he said, 'Give me just one more second.' He didn't shut up back then either. He wanted one more second, and he wanted me to hear him breathe, and was ready to let me know that the pace of his breathing had changed.

'All happy?' he repeats.

'Not while you're alive,' Nadia murmurs.

I look at her again. She smiles back, shrugging.

'So happy,' Carla responds with sarcasm.

They laugh, hold hands. I see the strawberries of Nadia's bra rot. They smell of the man sitting next to me on the plane here.

'Why don't we go and find Karl's room later?' Nadia whispers. 'Can't be that hard.'

'Deal. We'll go when everyone's asleep,' Carla says.

I ask myself if I should tell Rachele, protect their body, which is my body too. Protect their sleep, which I'm guessing is my sleep too. I look at Carla and Nadia, their hands held so tight, then turn away and look up at the sky.

'Tonight is our night,' Carla repeats.

I breathe in all of the darkness, and all of this cold. Is tonight our night? I stare into the void, the moon, and the million snowflakes, feeling hungry as a wolf. I wish I'd had that pizza. I walk faster so as not to think about it. Then to the bus. And to try to be alone again.

'You can't run away forever, Marti,' Nadia says, laughing. 'There's nowhere to go, anyway.'

THURSDAY

I hear a muffled scream. I try to bury myself in sleep but the noise doesn't stop. I open my eyes. Outside the moon is so bright it throws its light into the room. I can see Carla holding Nadia face down onto the mattress, her hands pushing into her neck. She is struggling for air and just about manages to free herself.

'I'll fucking kill you,' Nadia wheezes. 'Stop it.'

'You're the one who's got to stop,' says Carla. 'You hurt me, I hurt you.'

'Stop what?'

'Stop wanting *him*.'

So this is about Karl. I shut my eyes, try to zone out. They'll be laughing soon enough. Inside my head, I say my name twice, I touch the tip of my nose twice, hold my breath and count to thirty. Sixty. A hundred. Why the hell did Rachele give me the penance of sharing a room with them? I quietly do my movements – touching the linen, my forehead, then the linen followed by my nose – times two, then times two and another two. The repetition works, slowing down my heartbeat.

Just as I'm drifting off, I hear Nadia gasping for air again. I sit up. I need to remind myself that I exist and I need to remind them too. That I can hear everything – *everything*, always – and counting isn't enough and won't make me disappear. If I had that power, I would have disappeared already, right? From Alex. Rachele. And probably from my entire life. But guess what, I'm still here.

'What's happening?' I say. 'Nadia, are you OK?'

'Mind your own fucking business,' Carla says. 'How *dare* you speak to us.'

My heart is about to explode, my hands are sweating. My head is full of things and words and noises, thuds and whispers I don't want, or need, or understand.

'Yeah, *Martina*,' says Nadia. 'Fuck off back to sleep.'

No, I think. No and no twice. No and no forever.

'You both fuck off,' I hear myself say. 'You stop. You shut up.'

A silence fills the room like a canyon, so deep, so gigantic, we could fall into it. Even the moon seems less bright. Maybe my anger is making everything darker, everywhere. Maybe when I'm in Romania, Romania goes dark too.

'Fuck off,' I repeat, louder this time.

They'll probably kill me, I think. I'll be dead and done for. I'll die in my stupid pyjamas, and someone will find my body with its absurd red hair, while I have achieved nothing in my life. I will not own a gym in shades of purple. I won't ever have been to America, India, or Africa.

I will never wake up under a torrential monsoon in Bangkok. Or nail a *Yurchenko 2.5*. I'll die as uselessly as I have lived while still sucking at the balance beam.

'Wow,' Carla whispers.

'Unreal,' says Nadia.

I realize that something worse than death could happen to me. The girls could decide to break my arm or my knee, and sew up my mouth to stop me talking. I get a flashback to the day Carla and Nadia grabbed Anna in the middle of the changing room and pushed her in the communal showers. Carla had accused Anna of badmouthing her to the rest of the team. To be fair, Anna had said that Carla was a bully. She was right and had just tried to be brave, to speak out. Carla *is* a bully. But in a team you shouldn't speak out, you should resist, get stronger, forget. Stay silent. And that day too, we learned the lesson.

'Did you really think I wouldn't find out?' Carla asked her. 'Or that anyone would believe you rather than me? You need to behave.'

I'd looked at Carla's mouth, and heard Alex's voice instead. Were those the same words he had used with her? She did behave accordingly.

'You need to be a good girl,' Carla said. 'Not go around destroying me and our team.'

Naked under the jet of ice-cold water, Anna begged for forgiveness as Carla sprayed shampoo into her mouth, squirting it out like it was sauce, right down her throat.

When I said, 'Stop it, Carla,' I did it quietly, because I was scared.

Carla took no notice anyway, shampooing Anna's hair, rubbing it in harshly, the water still freezing cold, and telling her how revolting her hair was and how come she wasn't ashamed to walk around with it being so filthy, her face being so embarrassing, her soul being so disloyal. But then her voice had switched and her anger seemed at once fierce and lovable. It was the sweetest voice I had ever heard.

'I'm going to take care of it and make you presentable, OK?'

'OK,' Anna said. 'Thank you for your help.'

'It's my duty. And my pleasure.'

I cried because I couldn't stop Carla. I cried because Anna was grateful for her punishment. And because Nadia didn't show any discomfort watching Anna's pain and fear.

'I am so sorry your mother doesn't love you because you're ugly,' Carla said. 'And I am so sorry that she prefers her poodles to you because their fur is softer than your hair. It's not your fault, OK?'

'Yes,' said Anna. 'You're right.'

'I'll help with that absence of love too,' said Carla, her tone even gentler. 'I love you. We love you. If you want, I'll kill her dogs for you.'

'Thank you but no,' Anna said. 'They can live.'

'Well, let me know if you change your mind,' Carla said, kindness now dripping from her mouth.

Carla took Anna's hand and led her back into the changing room, where she dried her body and hair like a caring mother, a caring friend, a caring teammate. They hugged.

That day, I went back home and again I asked if I could leave the team and train with another coach and in another club. But my parents, tired and weak, repeated their mantra of the tired and of the weak, and said that it was too complicated, pointless, and unexpected and was it a mega problem if I were to stay? Their faces were those of people who knew nothing. I couldn't stand looking at them. I nodded, and zipped up my tracksuit twice.

It wasn't a mega problem.

Today, in Romania, I guess I'm nodding again. And again I'm doing my ponytail twice.

'Fuck off,' I say, louder this time. 'Just fuck off!'

Romania freezes, the wolves are all staring at this side of the forest, in awe of my courage. The whole world is staring at this side of the forest in awe of my courage. From their king-size bed, the girls stare at me too. And after the emptiest and longest silence, I hear Nadia and Carla laugh. Belly-laughing, as if I have just been really funny. With the sound of their laughter, Romania starts breathing and moving again, and the wolves get back to their own business, dealing with their hunger and with their team games. Eating other animals. Trying not to be eaten by other animals.

'Well done, Martina,' Carla says. 'Impressive. You might want to put that energy into vaulting.'

'Yes,' says Nadia. 'Use it for your *Tsukahara*. We like you, warrior.'

'Now, though,' says Carla sharply, 'go back to sleep and leave us the fuck alone.'

I lie down feeling proud. But also sad for being proud because of a 'fuck off'. I try to slow my heartbeat and get rid of the adrenalin clogging my muscles. It's toxic – the room, Carla, Nadia, the need to spit out poison in order to save myself. I count five, six minutes, second by second, and my breathing gets fuller, taking me away, millions of light years from here. I can still hear Carla and Nadia whispering, I can still hear the duvet rustling, then I hear them kissing. In my haze I imagine their tongues being really long and their boyish bodies naked in the snow. I nestle into that kiss. And in that nestle I sleep.

When I open my eyes again it's still night and their bed is empty. I get up and feel their duvet to check they aren't still under it. I look in the bathroom, in the closet. In my head I hear Rachele's voice asking for my help. Then I hear my voice asking for her help. One body, one heart.

Putting on my tracksuit and puffer jacket, I open the door and peer into the corridor. It's empty and in the empty corridor I see my future implode. Even this one second spent here, and the interruption of my sleep, is putting my performance in jeopardy. My concentration for the individuals will be fucked, my future in a national team will be fucked too. I have worked for years to be here and I'm not getting the sleep I need, and I'm not thinking of the things I need to be thinking about. I am walking around a hotel in the middle of the night, on the top of a mountain, because of a pair of evil and selfish idiots. I keep repeating to myself that I'm doing it for Rachele, for the team. For myself. That it's my duty to look after Carla and Nadia so we can all be on the path to glory. So we can all be safe.

I step out into the corridor. It is so silent and still, I can hear the lift humming. As I go down the service stairs, I'm filled with dread at the thought of bumping into Rachele and some lover of hers. Maybe Carla is right, and Rachele does get up to porn things at night. I don't see anyone and when I reach reception, I open the door facing the forest. Have they gone out into the night? For one of Carla's bets? Outside it's dark and freezing, at least minus one million degrees. I see their footsteps in the snow. My feet sink into them, one after the other, and my heart feels like it's about to explode.

I hear howling and I pray it's the wind and not a wolf. 'I know I said I wanted to live with you guys,' I say towards the forest, 'but maybe not tonight?'

The bridge to the gym looks a lot further away than it did this morning. I start running but I keep sinking in the snow, and I can feel my hands, my face, and my toes turning to ice. From here, the sports centre looks like a sci-fi town where the rules of life are different, harder. And secret. I keep on walking and see myself falling off the vault tomorrow morning, then slipping on the beam because my hands have been damaged by the cold and by my wrong decisions. I have never felt as far from the Olympics as tonight. I see myself dead near the uneven bars. Then dead in this darkness.

I run more and I know I should turn around and go back to the hotel, and my duvet. Instead, I keep running until I get to the sports centre and slip through the open door where the heat welcomes me and the roof seems to protect me. I hear distant sounds coming from inside the arena. I tiptoe forward, trying to breathe quietly like a spy. I push open a door, pressing half an eye and half my nose into the tiny crack. But it's all switched off in here, the uneven bars are empty, and the rings are hanging still. For a moment, I think about slipping in and practising my routine, the turning headstand, the grips. I could go through all the movements singing or shouting, with no one's eyes on me, no judgement, no scores. Remember my dream. The reason I'm here.

I hear a noise and I turn my head towards it. I see that Nadia and Carla are in the furthest corner lying on the balance beam, one on top of the other. It seems like there's no gravity over there, and they are weightless, and free. They really are one body and their body seems to be strong and indestructible. Then I spot Karl.

The three of them are now laughing as I watch him move onto the mat. He starts tumbling, imitating Nadia's floor routine first, then goes straight into Carla's. I can't believe his accuracy, how he nearly knows their choreography by heart. Nadia laughs and claps at Karl's almost-perfect technique, then stops when Carla moves away from her and gets on the mat. There, she gets into the bridge position and climbs onto Karl. He touches her arms, her shoulders. Both of the girls go and hang from the uneven bars, side by side, thighs touching. Karl gets up from the floor and goes over to them. Their eyes close as Karl strokes their legs, his hands as far up as their leotards. First he does it with his hands, then with his mouth. Carla is doing all she can to become the centre of attention. She passes her tongue across her lips. She calls him back anytime he goes to Nadia. She kisses him. Then she quickly kisses Nadia. I hold my thighs really close together to try to feel what they are feeling. Nadia tilts her head back and her mouth falls open. I think I hear her go 'Ah' in one exhalation, so I try to do the same.

'Ah,' I whisper.

When she lifts her head back up I realize she is looking at me. She doesn't say anything, the expression on her face hardly changes, but I'm scared and I flee. Outside it is darker, colder, it is now at least minus ten million degrees, and the distance between the gym and the hotel seems ten million times longer, my legs ten million times shorter.

'You can't run away forever, Martina,' I say to myself as I run in the snow. I fall and I run more.

Back at the hotel I run straight into the lift. My cheeks are stinging and I feel feverish. I get to the fifth floor and as I stand in front of Rachele's room, ready to knock,

I don't know what to do. Or say. I press my ear to her door and try to make out any noises coming from inside. But no noises are coming from inside. I knock so lightly that nobody answers. I did what I was asked and I wasn't heard. Story of my life, I guess. Story of her life too, I guess. And because it seems that the truth is that I can in fact run away forever, I run away once more.

I go back to my room, pull off my clothes, get under the duvet, and lie there shaking, counting how many seconds I can go without breathing and how many seconds it will take to get my feet to warm up again. I try to think of something else, anything but Nadia and Carla's bodies, Karl's hands, the wolves invading my brain. Is this what is happening to Nadia's brain when she sees things? To distract me I try to visualize the layout of each class I've been in, nursery, primary, and middle school. I place each one of my classmates in their own seat, each classroom on its own floor, in its own building and street. I try to place myself in those classrooms. In the world, and in this story.

I even try to smile for a picture no one is taking.

Maybe soon after or maybe much later, Nadia comes back. I wake up at once as she slams the door. She's crying, gasping for air, and goes straight over to the window. As she opens it icy-cold air comes in and I think I will never be warm again, until I leave this country. Or maybe this life. Then I see that Nadia is naked.

'Aren't you cold?' I ask.

She doesn't answer but she shuts the window. She gets into her bed, still crying and shaking. Did Karl rape her? Did Carla and Karl rape her, one after the other? Why am I even thinking about rape? You see a lot about rape on TV and maybe it has actually happened to her. Or maybe it's just me being obsessed, not able to leave words like rape or thoughts of Alex behind.

I rub my feet against each other twice. I blink twice, then twice again.

'Is Carla still at the gym?' I ask.

I'm still deciding which words to use with Rachele tomorrow, when Carla steps in. I check the time. It's half past five.

'Thanks for leaving me behind,' she says. 'What the fuck?'

Nadia doesn't move. I stay still too, pretending to sleep.

'I'm talking to you,' Carla says, undressing.

But Nadia doesn't reply and Carla appears to fall asleep the moment her head hits the pillow.

When, at seven thirty the next morning, we are putting on our leotards and pulling up our ponytails and fixing our hair buns, Nadia is still not speaking to her. Did they have a fight at the gym? Was it Karl's fault? These thoughts are making me lose all of my focus on the day of the individual qualifications. I cannot afford this distraction. I put my earphones in, and put the music up as loud as possible.

We have our mini breakfast, spit the food we secretly have to spit, and pop the pills we secretly have to pop, then we go to the gym. During the warm-up Nadia sits next to me, without uttering a word. Her movements are so soundless it's like she's floating, hovering half a centimetre above the floor, the chair, and above us all. We stretch and together we do our ab crunches. Then, mouths shut, we do our squats and burpees. Maybe from today we both will be the silent gymnasts and maybe we could be a new duo.

Carla sits by herself, her face crumpled with sleepiness, fresh red blotches on her cheeks. Rachele keeps asking her if she is feeling well. If she is feeling feverish. Sick in any way?

'Have you eaten something that's disagreed with you, Carla?' she asks.

'I'm fine thanks. What about you, Coach? How are you feeling?'

'I'm fine,' says Rachele, irritation and concern in her expression.

'You look a bit fatter, you know? I don't mean to be rude. But your bottom really looks bigger nowadays.'

Rachele pulls up her tracksuit as if suddenly remembering that she has a backside. I wish I could tell her I too have become aware of my cellulite since Carla has said the word cellulite and Nadia has been seeing images of Angelika being tortured and killed in every possible way for three days now, just because Carla has said the word torture. So we really are one body and one heart but we have to always remember that we are one mind too. And anyway Rachele still has a nice figure, very feminine, and the tracksuit actually sort of suits her. Maybe she could just stop having pasta at dinner, for a month or so.

'Benedetta,' says Carla. 'Help me stretch.'

Benedetta blushes as she sits on Carla's back. Only Nadia has ever been allowed to sit on Carla's back. This, I notice, scares Rachele more than anything she has seen up until now. We pretend this doesn't terrify us too. We take off our tracksuits and are about to start our individual qualifications, when Carla comes over to Nadia. I stare straight ahead, trying to look invisible, and as though I don't have ears.

'Why did you run away last night?' Carla asks Nadia. 'What the fuck is wrong with you?'

Nadia doesn't look at her and doesn't answer.

'Are you *stupid*? What's with the silence and the attitude?' Carla asks. 'We searched everywhere for you.'

Carla isn't getting anything from Nadia, so she starts with their 'Red red yellow blue – Coca-Cola Fanta glue – teeth straight feet straight – me me but it's you – blue pooh Fanta glue – I protect and so do you.'

Still nothing happens.

She tries two, three times more, hoping Nadia will join in. Then she looks at Nadia, challenging her with a death stare. The rest of us are spellbound. Rachele is covering her mouth with her hand, as if something really tragic has just happened. As if one of us has fallen off the bars and is being taken away on a stretcher. Or as if a physiotherapist has been sticking his fingers into our vaginas since we were 10, 11, 12, 13 and it was considered just fine.

Nadia does not break the stare.

'You're dead to me,' Carla says. And walks away.

Once – when they were 11 – Nadia had refused to wear a skirt to a gymnastics Federation party. Carla wanted her to wear one just like hers, telling Nadia it was a matter of principle because she had nice legs, even if they were 'a little short'.

'I don't want to wear a skirt,' said Nadia. 'Your wanting me to is becoming an obsession.'

'So come in your tracksuit,' Carla replied. 'You'll look great.'

'I don't want to come in my tracksuit. I want to wear trousers.'

Nadia won the battle; they didn't speak for half a day or so, but through their mantra and a few other stupid jokes they made up. Another time they had a row because

Carla had given Nadia a shove to wake her up during one of her stuck moments. Nadia had reacted badly when Carla called her *demented* and *loser* – but that was that. I can remember only silly things like these, which would be forgiven straightaway. And it was Carla who would always say or do something silly to make Nadia laugh. Rachele would laugh, we would laugh too. Carla was our Popeye. She was strong, had huge biceps, and always won.

But today it's different. Today Nadia doesn't say 'red red yellow blue', and this is such a serious snub that I almost feel like reciting the rhyme in her place. How can Nadia leave Carla in this state? How can she do this to us, to the team? After all her theories about statistics and superstitions! We hate the rhyme, we hate the sodding blue pooh, but reciting their mantra now, during this competition, during *any* competition, is compulsory.

Carla swallows the humiliation, then flexes her back a couple of times. She goes to the bars, breathes in, smiles, and jumps to grab the lower bar. Nadia keeps looking down at her feet, her lip trembling, her chest going quickly up and down. She only tilts her face once, to look at Karl, who has stepped into the arena, so she doesn't see that when doing the *Bardwaj* Carla loses her grip. And falls. She doesn't see when Carla stands up, touches her left knee, and gives Rachele a long look as if to say that something is wrong. I feel the pain in Carla's left knee and grit my teeth.

'Up,' Rachele mutters.

'Up,' we all mutter.

Carla jumps up again and Rachele watches her best athlete hesitate during her routine at the bars then again at the beam. Her movements and her scores today are average, her rhythm and elegance a pale reminder of the girl everyone saw yesterday. Today she's not God's angel. Angelika is beating her on everything. All the Chinese girls and Nadia are beating her too. I, incredibly enough, do better than her both on the beam and on the floor routine.

Rachele marches towards me. She too must be thinking about blue pooh and that after years of work, all is going to shit. I zip and unzip, and I have to do it ten times before being able to breathe properly again, while the other coaches fix their eyes on us and gloat. Or so it seems to me. Rachele drags along that enormous backside of hers. It probably now weighs around one hundred thousand kilos. Skipping pasta at dinner might not be enough. Or maybe she could just embrace this new body, eat more and more pasta and more of everything, always, become titanic and powerful and strong. Being as vast as, let's say, the stratosphere, she could shout more, crush us better, be more scary. It would be very straightforward. It would be honest. We would recognize the monster better. And we'd know better who we need to kill.

After her loose vault, we all see Carla's success at Sunday's All Around vanish.

'Martina, what's happening?' the monster hisses.

'I don't know, Rachele,' I say, my heart hammering, my legs shaking.

'What happened last night?'

'I slept.'

I look at Nadia then at Carla. I go through the speech I have prepared for our coach – their disappearance, Karl, the fight, Nadia's pain – and decide to forget it. I didn't ask to be put in Nadia and Carla's room. It's not my place to sort them out. I've done OK at the beam, I got a 14.20. I can't complain. She can't complain. I actually feel like telling Rachele to fuck off too. What if that was to be my abracadabra for all things in life?

'Martina, we must get to the Olympics. Right?'

'Right.'

'And we also know that Carla must get up there on the podium at the All Around. And Nadia must be in the first ten too.'

'I don't know what to say, Coach.'

I see the last tiny bit of love Rachele has for me evaporate. To make it easier to hate her back, I picture her thighs full of cellulite, fat holes, like Carla said. I imagine her getting older, weaker, and looking at me with that fake smile of hers. I add a stinky fag to her decrepit face, to her lifeless lips. In my thoughts she is 80 or maybe 1,000 years old.

'I'll take care of it, Marti,' she had told me. 'Just don't tell anyone else. For the club's sake, OK?'

I waited. Hopeful.

'She told me not to tell anyone else, for the club's sake,' Nadia said to me.

So we both waited. Hopeful. It was for the club's sake.

I walk towards Nadia. She's crying even though she's just done more than OK at the floor routine. She is fourth. Carla is behind her.

'Do you want some water?' I ask.

She nods, so I give her my bottle. She cries more so I worry more.

I never worry when it's me who cries. I know that even if I'm crying, I can deal. Be a pioneer of my pain. But when I see other people cry, I feel they must be really desperate and that they're so unhappy they might kill themselves. When my mum cries for example, I'm so scared I could pass out. Once, when we were doing the cleaning in an advertising agency at five in the morning, I caught her crying while she was dusting and it was the most unhappy hour of my life. Outside it was freezing and the streets were empty. I had climbed up on a desk and was watching the traffic lights flash amber. In terms of sad nights, we'd seen much worse. We'd cleaned old people's homes. And hospitals. But in that office, seeing her cry made it the saddest hour and turned the night into the saddest ever. I had looked at the street below and the city doing its best to go dark. I did it so as not to embarrass her, and tried distracting myself by thinking of the houses where people slept while we were working, searching for a way to make her happy, even here, with the window cleaning spray in one hand and the duster in the other. I looked for a way for us to save ourselves. But she was crying too hard, so eventually I did look at her and she explained she wasn't sad, only tired. It was like she had to justify herself to me. Had I not been there, had I been invisible, she could have cried without feeling embarrassed or guilty.

'Why can't I sleep at home and stay with Dad?' I'd heard myself say. I wanted to be sweet but I could only be bitter.

'Dad starts his shift at four in the morning.'

'I hate you,' I said. 'I hate both of you.'

But it wasn't true. I could have said 'I love you' and I don't know why I said 'I hate you'. On the bus back home, she fell asleep with her forehead against the window.

'It's not true that I hate you,' I said.

'I know,' she mumbled. Her mouth was dry, her skin so grey.

I snuggled under her armpit and slept, thinking of a way to save her. Then me. To this day my plan remains the same blurry one that involves gymnastics and glitter on the eyelids and sometimes in my hair.

Nadia and I watch Carla talking to Rachele, her head bowed.

Even when she's crying Nadia is prettier than me, no contest. I stare at her lips. At her tears, which make her cheeks pinker. We watch Alex approach Carla and Rachele. He seems genuinely concerned. I have to admit he might love this sport. And I bet he has a blurry plan for the future just as I do. The home-made video of some chiropractor working a girl's spine somewhere in Nevada must be part of it.

'What is it, the knee?' he asks Carla.

She nods and sits on the floor, to let him work on her leg and spray her with the dry ice.

'Better?' he asks.

'Worse,' she says. 'You've touched it.'

When she comes back towards us, Carla sits down next to Anna. Benedetta makes room for her and a Carla-place is instantly created on the bench.

'Did Karl rape you?' I ask Nadia.

She stares at me for a few seconds, disgusted, her fore-head shining with sweat.

'Or are you sad because Carla wants to steal Karl away from you?'

She looks at me with hatred now, then probably finds it tiring, gets up, and goes to sit further away. Full of her hate and my hate for myself, I go to the vault and nail two perfect jumps. While I fly and twist, I think *Fuck off, Carla. Fuck off, Nadia. Fuck off, Alex and Rachele.* I think it with utter conviction and the more I think it, the cleaner my moves become. I do a round-off on the springboard, pre-flight, first flight. I nail a

Yurchenko full and a half. I land. I salute. I fuck them all off once more in my head and suddenly see myself making it to the first ten at the All Around. I even dare to see myself at the Olympics.

I smile, while outside it starts snowing again and I decide there and then, that fuck off will be my favourite mantra forever. The more I look at the snow, the more I also think I need to go north to countries like Finland, Sweden, and Norway. And Iceland: where there are no trees but volcanoes so powerful they can ground planes and hot water with geysers and natural milky-blue pools. I'll go there when I can drive and like Goldilocks I will try them all and choose one that will be the perfect one. I will build a wooden cabin next to it. I will have a fireplace in the bedroom. All the wolves of Iceland will be my friends too.

I put my earphones in and lie down on the bench, watching the beautiful Romanian girls in their beautiful leotards do routines that are more beautiful than ours. I see Angelika being a million times better than Carla. And anyone. I spy Karl with his gelled hair who is looking over at Carla while also eyeing up a Polish gymnast with decent-sized boobs. I see Benedetta failing one movement after the other.

'I suck,' she says. No one dares contradict her.

Nadia is still crying and Carla is plaiting Anna's hair. It kills me that Anna is looking so grateful, her bright pink cheeks on fire with happiness. I want to go over and remind her of the times Carla has hit her or humiliated her. The time she told her that her father was always away because her mother was a dog.

'Like mother, like daughter,' she said.

But I pull my zip down and up to stop myself from

spoiling her party. Even though I know that later Carla will wash her hands to rid them of the feel of Anna's hair.

'It was like touching vomit,' she'll say. Or maybe she'll say 'like touching crap'. Or shit. Or saliva.

We close with our floor routines. We are all clean and precise, even if Carla is uninspiring and even if we are all downhearted. We pray for the other girls – especially the Romanians, the Chinese, and the Russians – to do badly, just to make us look better. And we pray so hard that apart from Benedetta, we all qualify for the All Around individual finals. For the others it was sort of obvious, for me it's a mega win. I will be competing among the best gymnasts at this tournament. And despite the pain for today's darkness, my heart is about to explode. I am instantly so happy that I want to scream. The idea that Nadia and Carla are weaker than usual, thanks to the fact that they are angry and distracted, suddenly seems appealing too.

That evening in our room, Nadia moves her bed away from Carla's, and she begs me to swap with her. Carla is still having her physio session with Alex, then she'll be in Rachele's room for the ice bath.

'I want to be near the window,' Nadia says.

'But what if Carla gets cross?'

'Shut up, OK? I don't care what she wants.'

We strip the beds and swap sheets. I lie down and stay still, as if I'm dead, as invisible as possible. I shut up. A corpse. A stone. When Carla returns she's ice-cold and silent. Maybe the ice bath froze her heart too. Maybe we will all be silent eventually.

I spend the evening with them on either side of me. Nadia watches videos on YouTube with her earphones in. Carla is restless. She puts on make-up. She takes it off. Then applies it again. I pick up my history textbook and read stuff about the Iron Age, the Golden Age, and whatever comes next. I'll never remember any of it and the teachers will never really test me on any of it. The schools we go to are so easy, we attend them just because it's the law. We need to train, that's our duty, and the teachers know it. They don't really care about me knowing anything. I am reading just to keep my eyes moving, my head occupied, my soul elsewhere.

Carla waxes her legs, then applies a face mask.

'I'm going out tonight, I need to have some sort of good time,' she says. 'When it's covered with snow, the village looks like Paris.'

She tears off a strip at the edge of her groin. Another one, on the other side. She cannot go out. And cannot have some sort of a good time.

'Please don't,' I say. 'You need to rest.'

'Do you want me to show you how to wax?' she says.

I've always shaved with a razor, in the shower, because this is how my mum taught me. Besides, she always says, it's cheaper. Once she also said something awful about how the wax makes your skin saggy in the bikini area. But Carla's mum is a beautician, so she must know and waxing must be better. I don't trust my mum: she always says we are happy and then she cries. Why should she be reliable on groins? Thanks to the beauty salon, sometimes after a shower Carla spreads mud over her body to prevent cellulite, wrapping herself in cling film. She smells of rosemary and mud. It's all stuff her mum has nicked, like the hairclips she and Nadia have in their hair, the paper knickers and nail varnish in all sorts of colours she has in her make-up bag. I wonder if Carla's mum, who is so religious, does penance for being a thief. I imagine the words she uses at night to talk to God, about anti-cellulite mud and her desire to own nail varnish in every shade.

'Karl is going to show me around,' Carla is saying to me.

I try not to add anything. I just know I have to stop looking at Carla and Nadia as if they are characters in a movie, a mystery to be solved, the grammar of a foreign language I'll eventually learn. I concentrate on the wallpaper, on the history book and all its ages and stages. I flip from page forty-two to page forty-three. Then forty-four.

'Are you listening to me, Martina?' says Carla. 'Look at me.'

I look at her. She is pushing her leg behind her ear, tearing off hair from a spot on the back of her thighs. I didn't even know there were follicles there.

'You can't go,' I tell her again. 'It's the finals tomorrow. The Romanians are ahead. So are the Chinese. We need you at your best. Angelika was perfect today and you weren't.'

'I'll fucking destroy her,' she says. 'I'll add a *Khorkina* and a *Kim*, no worries.'

'You haven't tried the *Kim* enough. Don't.'

'Shut up.'

'Nadia saw Karl before you,' I blurt out.

Carla bursts out laughing. But her eyes aren't laughing. Nadia still has her earphones in and I wonder if she really is oblivious to what we're talking about. She's never looked so small.

'Do you have chairs and meat and a TV at home?' asks Carla. 'Or can you not afford them?'

'We can't afford them. So what? Nadia liked Karl first,' I repeat. 'Also, she's clearly not well.'

'I like him too and there are things you don't know. And you don't know them, because who'd tell you anything?'

'You. You're talking to me. Now.'

'Your voice is weird,' says Carla. 'And if you ever tell me to fuck off again, I'll kill you.'

All dolled up with blue eyeshadow and pink nail varnish, she leaves the room. Nadia puts her face in her pillow. I go to watch Carla from the window as she crosses the snow-covered yard. I don't think she really is as cruel as she'd like me to think. I don't think she's kind either but as I watch her stumble and rub her eyes, I feel sad for her. In the snow, near the forest, I see Angelika doing her solo night training. Then I see Karl run and catch up with Carla. I have to retie my ponytail twice before I can move away from the window and convince myself that my voice is not weird. And that I don't have to go and tell Rachele that she's gone. I go and sit near Nadia. Her bed seems the loneliest spot in the Milky Way. Like it's floating, alone, in nothingness.

'Are you OK?' I ask her.

'Yes,' she says.

And she hugs me. She can't be OK if she's hugging me. Also, her body is shaking.

'Shall I switch off the lights?'

She nods, grateful, and turns her back to me. I put my earphones in and hope not to hear any other sound until morning. But when in the middle of the night I open my eyes, I catch a glimpse of Nadia through the bathroom door as she is inserting a tampon. So she's started her periods and already knows how to use a tampon. Maybe she's watched her mother. I wouldn't know how to use one and I hope I don't have to for months. Years, possibly. I'll just have to cut out more food to make sure.

Nadia wipes a tiny spot of blood off the bathroom floor and drops the stained toilet paper in the loo. As I am watching I already know this is one of those moments that will stay in my memory forever. There's nothing I can do about it, it will be right there, along with a couple of fights with my mum, the sound of Alex when he comes, and learning the colour of a dead girl's skin. All the details will be mixed up, forever, together with some fears I had when I was 3 or 4 and the sound of that time I fell off the beam and banged my head so hard I passed out.

FRIDAY

I get out of the shower and dry myself with the stiff towels that could help the Polish girl with the yellow acne. When I step into the bedroom, Nadia is not there anymore. I didn't hear Carla come back last night but here she is now, half leaning out of the window, spitting and most probably aiming for Angelika's head. She turns around, wraps herself in the curtains, and smiles at me, a thread of saliva on her chin. She wipes it off with her wrist then spits again in my honour, louder, like smokers do in the street. I'd love to be able to hawk like that.

Her phone rings.

'Hi, Mum,' she says. 'Yes, I'm doing great. Loving it here.'

She rolls her eyes. As far as I can see she isn't doing great at all. She also looks tired.

'What?' she says. 'I'm fine. I don't know what Rachele told you, but I'm fine. I promise. Yes, Mum. I love you too.'

She winks at me. Pretends to vomit.

'Yes, Mum. I'm the best. The Lord, yes. We love him forever and ever.'

She ends the call, zips up her tracksuit. I do the same. Then I zip it down and back up again.

'Aren't you gonna ask me if I had fun last night?' she says. 'If I had sex?'

'Did you have fun last night? Did you have sex?'

She nods and brushes her hair. I am not sure if nodding counts as an actual yes, so I am not sure she really had sex. With Karl or with anyone else, ever. I focus on her hair, which is so long and blonde that if the Lord hadn't come into her life she'd be great for a shampoo ad.

'We went to the city centre and had a kebab. We also went to a bar to get a Coke. I think I saw Alex getting wasted.'

'I hope he dies.'

'Oh, Martina,' she laughs. 'Pretend he's just a nightmare. Then you'll wake up.'

'We'll never wake up. Not if we don't get rid of him.'

'We will. Eventually,' she says. She changes tack. 'When I got back you were snoring big time. Like a fat fifty-year-old man. I'm going to record you.'

'Did you speak to Nadia? She's not well.'

'Big news. Anyway, she left when I was sleeping. Not that she would have spoken to me anyway.'

'What's going on?'

'She's obsessed with me. You know it. I know it.'

'Thought it was about you stealing Karl from her?'

'I wish it was that simple,' she laughs. 'Shall we?'

We leave the room, Carla by my side. The way she is talking to me, you'd think we were friends. The way she smiles, you'd think we really are happy. But, as she says, nothing is that simple. I hope Nadia doesn't see us because she might think I'm on Carla's side. And if I had to choose, I'd still bet on Carla being guilty. But even guilt is not that simple.

'Fix your hair,' Carla tells me. 'You could be so pretty if you only put in the effort.'

So I fix my hair, and put in the effort.

In the reception area, some of the boys are lounging about on the sofas. They're ugly, all of them – spotty, short, or greasy-haired. And they smell. They smell more when they bathe themselves in cologne than when they sweat. We sit down without even saying 'hi'.

'The Polish girl is not dead,' one of them says.

I'd forgotten about the Polish girl. Am I so cruel that I haven't given more thought to the motionless body of a girl like me, being taken away on a stretcher, her neck in a brace, her feet stiff? If she had died and nobody had talked about her ever again, I would have probably been OK with it.

'Not even paralysed?' says Carla.

'Only injured,' another boy answers.

Only injured. And one less competitor.

We don't have anything to add. So we don't say anything and we just stay there, waiting for Benedetta, Nadia, Anna, and Rachele. Outside the glass doors, we watch two men shovel the never-ending snow from the hotel entrance. They pour salt on it, then they shovel some more, puffs of steam coming out of their mouths. They say something, then laugh. One of them is older than the other; maybe they are father and son. Their cheeks are red and their shoulders so wide, they look like bears in coats. I would like to say it out loud – *see those bears in coats?* – and for people to whisper 'what a cute sentence that was, Martina. What a cute soul you have, hon.' I would like to go there and help them. Instead, I retie my ponytail twice.

When she arrives, Nadia sits far away from us. Her forehead is damp with sweat. She is wearing sunglasses and has her earphones in. As Benedetta and Anna approach, I can see how they take in the enormity of Carla and Nadia's separation, while we all pretend it's nothing. Like when your parents fight and you know you can't ask, 'What happened?' It's their business and anyway the embarrassment shuts your mouth, scares you to death, and gives you a parent-fight type of tummy ache. I have different kinds of tummy aches. One for competitions, one for Alex, another one for when Nadia looks so ill. So today I go for this specific one and welcome its specific pain.

'Hi,' the Useless Ones say. And I am the only one who responds with a 'Hi' back.

Carla doesn't look at them nor at Nadia. Nadia doesn't look at Carla either. I look at both of them but once again I prefer the snow out there, the shovels and the laughter of the bears in coats. I wish there was no one fighting around me as making up can be really difficult and the sweat on other people's foreheads really troubles me.

'Did you go running in the forest?' Carla asks Nadia quietly. 'Did you see Angelika?'

Nadia doesn't answer. She rubs her hands and stares straight ahead.

My parents split up once. My mum said to my dad, 'You're a horrid human being.' Every time she walked into a room and he was in it, she shooed him away. He cried and said, 'I'm leaving because you hate me.' I looked at them through one eye, while the other eye stayed fixed on the TV. He moved out, onto Nino's couch. He came to my school once to hug me and he cried. At some point, weeks later, they made up and she was kind to him again. I'm not sure what happened in between, maybe just the passing of time, but something on Dad's neck looked bruised. Had he tried hanging himself? Had my mum tried to choke him? These were the first things that came to mind: suicide and homicide. No one spoke of it again. If they ever feel they should tell me why they got back together, it will be when I'm a grown-up, and I'll care even less and the back-drop to my life will be that of Los Angeles.

I'll be smiling, somewhere near the canyons.

Rachele comes into the lobby, her fringe the biggest, puffiest giant fringe in Europe. If she ends up in prison, I think there and then, she should do fringe tutorials online as a job. Three-minute videos, hairdryer extrava-ganza and all. Thumbs up. Thumbs down. She could nail it. She could go on with her theories on beauty and girls and bodies. People would comment, ask questions about the products she uses: *And the orange lipstick you always wear, what brand is it?* But today, after we have whispered nasty things about her mega-big bleached hair, we don't ask anything. We just fall silent again. She beckons us and we follow her to the usual physio check-up with Alex.

I go in first. I am the pioneer of the check-up.

'Forty-four kilos, one metre forty-eight, a hundred beats per minute,' says Alex.

Please let me go, I think. *Please die*, I also think.

'Heart's a bit fast. And you're getting taller. Anything else you want to tell me?'

'I'm fine,' I say. I am not. *I hate you.* And getting tall sucks.

'Nervous about the championship?'

'I'm fine.'

'Hang in there and be brave.'

'I'm being brave now, here, with you,' I manage to say.

I count to five. Then to ten. I try not to meet his eyes while he checks my blood pressure, then my bruises. He quickly manipulates my left ankle. I move my left ankle away. I stand up.

'If I say "Martina", what do you say?'

He wants to sound normal but his voice is cracking. He is trying to follow his script. I hate his script. I hate his script, I hate his hands, his mouth, his penis, which I have seen get hard in his pants tens of times. I hate his smell, his voice, his hair. His name.

'I say winner?' I mutter.

I manage to look him in the eyes. He lowers his. Piece of shit.

'OK, Martina. You're a winner. You can go now.'

I am a winner. I can go. So I go.

Alex gives us a physio session daily, and a check-up every week. If we are travelling, the check-up can last less than six minutes. If you're quick at taking off your clothes and putting them back on, stepping onto the scales, standing up straight, and pretending to cough, it may last five minutes and that's it. I still haven't worked out what triggers him to touch us in the other way. The sick, disgusting, other way. I often wonder what drives him more. Is it our happiness or our sadness? His strength and our weakness? Or our strength and his weakness? Should I cry or smile when I'm with him to be safer?

'I know it can be uncomfortable,' he now sometimes says, after I complained to Rachele.

Somehow, speaking about it must feel more medical to him. More professional. He does the same with Nadia and Carla.

'I'm almost done,' he might add. 'Your hip needs fix-ing so that's where you have to work when you work on the hip.'

And he touches me, again, where – now I know – my hip that was never weak, or never broken, needs constant fixing. Nadia's problem seems to be the lower back. Carla's the knee and the shoulders. Somehow the nerve to work all of these broken bits of us is inside our vagina.

'Nothing is wrong with my lower back,' Nadia had told Rachele.

'Guys, he's the best,' she'd replied to her. 'He walked me through all of it. All is fine.'

I cannot 100 per cent say that she didn't believe him, or that with a tiny part of ourselves we didn't believe him either. We believed them. We desperately wanted to.

I leave the door open behind me and I sit outside. I can hear my team members being weighed and Alex's questions. I can hear how often he repeats 'Now you must eat a bit more. If you don't eat anything, you can't compete.' All of us are told the same in Alex's room, but less than half an hour later Rachele will tell us to cut our portions, our carbs, the sugars. Do they have an agreement on that too?

'You won't like how you look in your leotard,' she'll whisper. 'Trust me. No movement looks good if you have a chubby belly.'

Nadia goes in last. She walks in with her earphones still in, dragging the dirty heels of her trainers, taking her beautiful tormented face into the medical room. Even when she's furious, or ill, I always see her beauty first. But today, looking at Nadia's soaked shoes, I also see her having the same gaze as the crazy old lady in my neigh-bourhood who walks around with a doll in her arms.

Nadia looks as lost and lonely as her. As sweet and kind as her.

'Stop doing that,' Carla says, pointing at my teeth.

'Doing what?'

'Stop grinding them. And stop shaking or whatever the fuck you're doing.'

Nadia disappears inside. I wish I could go in with her.

'Nadia, you're making a mess on the floor,' I hear Alex tell her. 'How come your shoes are so filthy and wet? Have you been in the forest?'

'I needed a breath of fresh air,' she says, and her voice is dry. 'And to be alone.'

'You're not allowed. Always go with someone else.'

The door shuts behind her.

'Martina, control yourself,' Rachele says. 'Please.'

So I try to control myself and to stop shaking or whatever the fuck I'm doing. The walls are so shit-thin that from where I am sitting, I can still hear bits of Nadia's check-up. I hear her say she has started her period and tell Alex that no, it doesn't hurt. I am pleased she doesn't have period pains. She says she thinks her wrists feel weaker than usual. Here they come, I think, more stress fractures. We all know they will break us, eventually. Then, I hear a loud noise, like metal crashing to the floor, glass shattering.

Carla turns round to face Rachele.

'Why do you leave us alone with him?' she asks. 'You're just as bad as he is.'

Rachele stares at her, horrified. She goes into the room and closes the door. Carla gets up, but when she realizes I'm watching her, and the others are watching her too, she shrugs and sits back down. I try giving her a grateful look but she doesn't meet my eyes. She is pale. We are all pale. If one of us goes pale we all do. If one of us is in there with Alex, we all are.

Has Nadia killed him? Has she killed herself?

We are always afraid of suicides. As if they're a kind of flu we could catch if we're unlucky, and because we are between 14 and 16 years old. If we trust Nadia's loathsome statistics and those on TV, they seem to happen all the time. The figures are terrifying and always accompanied by descriptions of the scene. Belts hanging, pills on the floor, an uncle's gun that has gone *bang* with brains splattered on bathroom tiles. The number of uncles' guns that are around, Jesus! To these figures and to the belts hanging from showers, you have to add the anorexia deaths, which in a way are suicides too. Anorexics who don't die from vomiting or weighing under 26 kilos or from a heart attack, are more likely to kill themselves than the non-anorexics, and this too is another statistic I learned thanks to Nadia. It goes without saying that we, for the same reasons and for all the other reasons that Carla wants to pretend are nightmares from which we can wake up, are more prone to suicide.

Last year, a Chinese gymnast and a French gymnast killed themselves. Different months, different methods, but we studied both cases with great attention. The Chinese girl was found hanging in the boarding school where she lived. She was 13 and she used the bandages we wrap around our hands for the uneven bars. She tied them to the shower, climbed onto the towel rack, slipped her head through them, and let herself fall. When the news became public, it had already been two months since her death. Their team made a brief statement but we couldn't find any interviews on the internet. Not a coach, not a teammate saying anything out loud. Rachele explained that the Chinese are very reserved. I guess she could relate with the approach, the nuance one can give to the word reserved.

'They are lying,' Carla had said, 'like hell they're reserved.'

'They don't want anyone to know because otherwise the world would find out about the stuff that goes on over there,' Nadia added.

'They say athletes are sixteen when they are in fact twelve. They kill them and pretend nothing's happened. They die and nothing is said. Dogs!'

Rachele had waited for us to stop repeating the words 'dogs' and 'death', then got us to do a relaxation exercise she had learned at yoga. She explained we would repeat this exercise regularly; it was good for concentration and for relaxation.

'It helps when you're scared,' she told us. 'You learn to breathe more slowly, when your body wants you to breathe faster. In a nutshell, it helps *you* to be in charge, and not your fear.'

That week we did yoga, but soon Rachele forgot about it or thought that too many of us had fallen asleep, so we went back to traditional stretches. I still use bits of the exercise she taught us to survive some physio sessions.

Alex's door remains shut for a few minutes. When it opens Rachele comes out. We look at her. She tries to smile to reassure us, and I have to say her smile does, weirdly, make me feel calmer. Despite everything, I do love her and I know she loves us. I guess it's the same for kids whose mums beat them. They still love them, don't they? They'll still enjoy that one hug. They still only have that one mum. I watch her smile again, before she starts talking in the most serene tone of voice she can master.

'She fainted. Nothing to worry about.'

'Why did she faint?' Anna asks. 'Is she ill?'

'Low blood pressure. She's fine now.'

'But why did she have low blood pressure?' I ask.

'It just happens,' Rachele says. 'Nothing to worry about.'

Carla has tears in her eyes and when I notice she puts on her sunglasses. She looks like a celebrity. Or a mourner at a funeral. Or a celebrity mourning at a funeral. She walks towards the windows, Rachele follows her, and I look at them from the back, Carla with her shoulders slumping towards the ground and Rachele's moving up and down as she talks too fast, using way too many words. I want to shout, 'If you just shut up, Rachele, maybe Carla will talk to you. If you take a break, maybe she will tell you something. Stop going on about the Olympics. Stop going on about your plans! You and Alex should use fewer words, fewer looks, less of *everything*.' But of course I remain silent. I zip up my fucking fleece. I zip down my fucking fleece.

Alex comes out and says Nadia needs a couple more minutes. She is feeling better, but low blood pressure can do this. After fainting, you need to get up very slowly.

'If you've already had your check-up,' he tells us, 'you can go to the gym.'

Low blood pressure? She's never had that before. Did Nadia push Alex away as he touched her? Did he push her back? Has she found the strength to do what we've all yearned to do?

I go to the gym and concentrate as best as I can, despite replaying images of Nadia fainting, the saliva on Carla's chin, her real or fake hand-jobs on Karl, the tampons, the blood, the tears. I can't make sense of any of it. Nor put order to any of it. So I start repeating things twice, saying 'help' twice, 'Carla' twice, 'Nadia' twice and doing abs crunches, and stretching my legs on autopilot. By the time Nadia and Carla start warming up, I feel better.

The other teams arrive. The arena fills up. The competition needs to begin. The finals need to begin. So, despite never being less of a team, or never having felt less focused myself, I try my best, I do my best to be a pioneer and to be here now. When it's my turn I also manage to get a high score at the bars. I thank my anger for it but have to hate my anger soon after, when I fall off the balance beam for it. I hurt my ankle. I hurt my wrist. I hope the ankle isn't linked to the same nerve as my hips and that Alex won't need to fix it in the same way.

Benedetta is our weakest spot and confirms it today too. Carla, on the other hand, is being a diligent, talented gymnast, no doubt about it, but that's about it. No sparkle. No magic. Again she doesn't seem to be God's angel today. She doesn't seem to be a Popeye either. She's just one of the good girls.

'Be your best self,' Rachele tells her. 'Please.'

Her voice comes out more like a lamentation. She's losing her sparkle and magic too. Anna tries to help us with her average, diligent consistency, but we are all lacking strength, precision, and beauty. Nadia is still so fragile we cannot count on her, she shouldn't even be competing, and when I land badly at the vault I cry.

'Girls,' Rachele says. 'Be the winners that you are. This is a shit show.'

Once at a competition in Sydney, the athletes kept on making mistakes at the vault and at some point – when many of the girls had already landed on their knees – they realized it was the vault that was off by a few centimetres. Maybe there is something wrong with these Romanian beams too. I am also getting taller and this is horrible. Nadia is getting her periods and this too is horrible. Then again, what about Khorkina's height, she who we always thought was absolutely perfect? At least before she started calling other gymnasts who spoke out about abuse 'liars in search of fame'. But we all heard Khorkina had started training with a coach who used to beat her and who would sometimes not let her eat for a whole week. Despite the beating, and the hunger – or maybe because of them – she won nine golds, eight silvers, and three bronzes. So, she probably thinks it has all been worth it. Or at least, we guess that that is the lesson she wants us to learn from her. And today, when we all seem to be failing badly, I am not sure anymore of what we need either. More beating? More care? I watch Angelika's flawless jumps and twists at the other end of the gym. Her smile. Does her perfection come from love or hate?

I watch the Chinese team pile up points. The Russians too. I envy them and feel sorry for them, at the same time.

By noon we make it to fifth place and none of us beat Angelika on any of the apparatuses and throughout the entire competition. We don't make it to the podium. We don't make it to anywhere decent. We still have the individual finals and the All Around, but as a team we are crushed.

By the evening, on top of our club being placed fifth overall, Nadia and Carla still haven't spoken. The atmosphere between them is tense. The atmosphere of the entire universe is tense.

Back in our room Carla and I discuss calculations for the All Around on Sunday. Discuss is a big word; Carla is talking and I'm listening. She is determined she wants to try the *Produnova* vault. It's called the 'vault of death' for a reason, as it's nearly impossible to control the forward momentum of a handspring into a triple front flip before a completely blind landing.

'Better paralysed than a loser. I've got this,' she laughs. 'Martina, you've got this too.'

Every so often Nadia rolls over on her bed and snorts. She is still pale, she has barely spoken, and I haven't seen her eat.

'What happened in the room with Alex?' I ask Nadia.

'Nothing,' she mutters. 'I fainted.'

'You're obsessed with Alex,' Carla says to me. 'Stop it.'

'But look at us. We're a mess.'

'We're not,' Carla says. 'Just focus on how impressive you can make your floor exercise. You need points.'

'It's their fault,' I say. 'All of this. They are making us crazy.'

Nadia turns to me and by the way she looks at me, I feel it's the first time she seems to have heard me. My voice has made it to her brain. But her cry for help, the horror I can see appear on her face, is so vast and so dark, I can't look at her anymore. I turn to the window. I walk towards it and look out there, where things might be easier. I see the bears with the coats and I hope they are taking care of everything. At least better than us up here.

'If Angelika gets fucking lost and a few Chinese super robots get fucking lost, we can still make it,' Carla continues. 'Then I'll get myself a nice spread in *Playboy* just like Khorkina.'

'How old do you have to be to be in *Playboy*?' I ask, thinking what a lame question this is but trying hard to bring us back to something jolly. To us being girls who joke. Who care about joking.

And that is why, Nadia and I, dark circles under our

eyes, stare at Carla doing a *Playboy* pose, rolling her T-shirt up over her tiny tits so they are showing better. She then lies down and poses with her back arched like a siren. Her arms are muscular and her skin is covered with bruises. She lets herself be watched so brazenly, I feel embarrassed.

'I'm going for a walk,' I say. 'Just to the vending machine and back.'

'You love me bad,' Carla says nastily to Nadia. Nadia shoves her face back against the mattress. 'Get me a Coke,' Carla adds. 'And get yourself some stronger moves for the beam!'

I think about Nadia loving Carla bad. She'd just lifted her face off the mattress and now we've lost her again. Carla is an idiot and I have a feeling she knows it.

'Did you know that if you douche with Coca-Cola you don't get pregnant?' Carla tells me.

'Could you be pregnant?'

'What the fuck are you talking about, Martina? Get me a Coke, will you?'

As I open the door she changes pose. I see her pulling her T-shirt back down and lying there, pretending to be bored. Then getting on all fours. As I shut the door behind me I hear her call Nadia twice.

I go to the vending machines and get Cokes for us and a Fanta for Nadia. She hasn't eaten anything so some sugar will do her good. I send Dad a text and write, Keep concentrating on Sunday! It's still our lucky day, isn't it?

I get his answer in two seconds. Sunday Revolution and Wonder. The cards are favourable. Luck! Ps: kisses from Mousy Mum.

As I walk back I hear noises coming from Anna and Benedetta's room. Music and laughter. The Useless Ones, the girls in the shadow, have their moments of happiness and have a soundtrack for it. It must be way more relaxing in there than with Nadia and Carla. Maybe it's because in there they are still safe. I walk further and get to Rachele's room. The door is half open so I stick my head through and I see her make-up and a few thin white cigarettes on a shelf. I can also see her reflection in the mirror. She's sitting in front of the TV, eating a chocolate bar, and she's crying. Then I see Alex, a towel around his waist, a little bottle from the minibar in his hands. He walks towards the door as I run away.

Back in the room, the first revolution has happened. I am tempted to call my dad and confirm his shamanic powers. Carla is now on Nadia's bed. Nadia's face is still buried against the mattress but Carla is embracing her from behind like one of those rucksacks in the shape of a cuddly toy that were fashionable when we were small.

Back then, I would have loved a panda backpack but there wasn't enough money. My dad had a go at making one out of those fluffy prize toys you get at a fairground shooting range, disembowelling it by pulling out the stuffing in its belly. He had made straps with a pair of old braces and the result was so sad I threw it in our outside wheelie bin at the first opportunity and pretended it had been stolen from the gym. A few months later I found it back in our flat, hidden in a bag of old things.

'You mustn't be sad,' Carla is telling Nadia. 'If you're sad I can't breathe or think straight. I can't jump or eat or sleep or anything.'

The list of things Carla can't do if Nadia is sad turns out to be so long I get pins and needles in my foot. I put the fizzy drinks on their bedside table and sit on my bed.

'I saw Rachele and Alex having sex,' I say.

'You didn't,' Carla says.

I realize I didn't.

'I saw Alex with no clothes on in Rachele's room.'

'Was he completely naked? Was his cock hard?'

I feel like fainting. I need some air.

'He had a towel round his waist.'

'So you didn't *see* them having sex. *Nor* was he naked.'

'What difference does it make? We should call the police!'

'Because maybe they fuck?'

'Because of what they do to us! Why would you ever protect them anyway?'

'I'm protecting the team, the medals. I'm protecting you!'

I look at Nadia, searching for a bond I don't find. She's under Carla's spell again. And she will be forever. I count to a hundred, two hundred. Nothing happens. Just the pins and the needles getting worse in my foot, then making their way up to my waist, my lungs. The tongue. My eyes.

'Come back, my love,' Carla is saying to Nadia. 'Can't you see without you I fail?'

During the pause that follows I switch off my bedside lamp, decide to forget them forever, and try to sleep. If they want to stay up tonight too, fine. I sure don't. If they don't want to call the police and become completely mad, fine. And if they don't believe me or don't ever want to speak about Alex, I don't care either. Maybe I can revise my mat routine in my head or think about some school stuff. Yes, some school stuff. English for instance. I am. You are. We are.

'Come back, my love,' Carla says again.

'Karl,' Nadia mumbles. 'He needs to go.'

'All right. Who gives a shit about Karl, anyway?'

Nadia turns her face, streaked with tears, and looks at

her best friend. Her love. My bed is in the dark while Nadia's is lit like a stage. I am the only spectator and I can't even clap.

'I will be really cold, a piece of ice,' Carla tells Nadia, her voice a bit elated. 'I won't even say hi to him. It was about you always.'

'I like that.' Nadia giggles. 'It was always about you for me too.'

'I'll cover my eyes with my hands every time he goes past. I'll run away every time he comes near me, like he's a bad smell. And I won't ever say any word starting with the letter K. I'll never say Karl again. Or king, Kraków . . . Kukaku!'

'Kukaku doesn't mean anything,' Nadia laughs. 'Kukaku doesn't exist!

'Kukaku is dead!' Carla shouts as she starts jumping on the bed.

'He is dead. The K is dead,' Nadia whispers.

They huddle together under the duvet, hugging and not talking any more, or maybe it's me falling asleep at last, with all the 'We are' and 'You are' I've been repeating to myself. Carla is never going to be able to say Khorkina again, if she means what she's promised.

But I decide not to point this out.

SATURDAY

They are both spitting out of the window, so I know things are better. And I know Angelika is down there running. Nadia is hugging Carla who seems to be back to her usual self. Their saliva is hanging down from their chins – like slugs' trails, shiny and white – and that counts as being back to their usual selves too. The sun is huge, phosphorescent yellow, and my heart weighs at least 100 kilos.

'Do you know what the only name more stupid than Angelika Ladeci is?' says Carla. 'Actually, it's so stupid I can't think of anything worse.'

'It's an old woman's name. And it's got a K in it, careful!'

'Right, that letter is dead. Why the fuck did I use it?'

I don't dare say Angelika Ladeci sounds like the name of a gymnast that will resound through the centuries. A name that's been around forever and will last forever.

Angelika Ladeci. Ladeci, Angelika: I can imagine her Wikipedia page with the list of the trophies she has won. Then all of the movements invented by her. I repeat her name and surname in my head until they lose meaning.

I get dressed and find a text from Dad. Mum and I are counting the hours till the All Around! To your competition and to your return. We are good here in the Mousy Mouse Land. I picture the sun in our suburb, also called the Mousy Mouse Land, hidden behind a static yellow mist. I picture them lost in that yellow mist, all mice and rats and litter around them. I try to hug them but even if it's an invented hug, I can't get myself to hold tight and I have to look up at the imaginary sky instead.

Before I started travelling, I used to think the sky was naturally faded blue, the sun always far away, just like at home. But then on our travels I began to see the sun for what it was and for what it could be, and my world back home became bleaker. Even here, in freezing Romania, the sun comes up cleaner, and larger, and it's so big it feels as if it's about to fall on you. It's so colossal it's easy to understand how much heat it can generate, and why it keeps us alive. Or sort of alive.

I brush my hair and it's so red it hurts. It's a fire and I can feel the heat. I zip up twice, down twice, drink two sips of water and try to forget about my hair and the heat on my skull and my forever untidy bun. I put on a smile and turn towards them.

'Shall we go and have our breakfast?'

'You're so common, Martina,' says Carla. 'Sophisticated people say *petit dejeuner*. That's what they'd call it at Anna's house.'

'Not that Anna would invite you,' says Nadia. 'Or us. Carla, could you give me a quick neck massage?'

When we were younger, we used to be invited to Anna's house a lot. Then the invitations stopped. I think it was after Carla tried on all her mother's shoes and left them scattered everywhere for the maid to pick up. Or maybe it was after Nadia and Carla got drunk on the liqueurs in the living room, and practised the routine from one of our old competitions, between the stairs and the basement, smashing a few vases along the way.

'Sorry, my love,' Carla said. 'Tell me if we owe you something.'

At Anna's house I discovered what real carpets were like and that there was a dryer that wasn't a washing machine. I learned of the existence of rooms that don't belong to anyone and stay empty, in which the beds are tidy and the sheets are clean and not one person sleeps in them. I imagined jolly ghosts, lying under the printed quilts, tapestries, and over them the softest blankets. It must be strange to change sheets that haven't been used, from beds that haven't been slept in. When do you do it? And why? Even if there was room for all her family, and spare people, it always felt empty. Her mother would come and go so fast it was like she was one of those cloaks magicians wear, with empty space underneath. We never saw her father but we heard words like 'diplomat', and 'girlfriends'. The kind of words that when put together explained why we never saw him and why Anna hated him.

The maid would come and tell us our snacks were ready, that they had put mats out in the garden for us to practise on, or that it was time for our bath and the bubbles were making it foamy. Anna was fond of the maid but Carla positively hated her. Even back then any maid would make me think of my mum, but Carla, bold and rude, just ordered her to bring her this and that. Or she would complain she was too cold. Then too hot.

'Maid!' she'd shout. 'What are you making for Princess Anna's dinner?'

And Anna would end up crying. But it was not like she had parents or someone that heard her.

In the canteen we sit with the rest of the team. Rachele starts smiling the moment she sees that Carla and Nadia are friends again. She's happy for Carla, our star, who now has her Nadia back, but more than anything she's happy for herself. So she starts talking as if she's never going to stop. Every so often, while she is going on and on, she winks at Carla. Or she says, 'Do you agree, Nadia?' And Nadia has to say, 'Yes, Rachele. I do.'

Turn it down a bit, I want to tell her as usual. *Turn it down, Coach, they're all looking at us, you are loud, you are bad*, but the blah blah has started; the tsunami of words cascading from her lipsticked mouth is in full swing. There is no way of stopping it.

Last night I saw you lying in front of the TV eating chocolate, crying, I'd like to say. *I saw you with Alex, he was naked – so despite all your words and this laughter, I don't trust you.*

But I remain silent. I redo my hair instead.

'I've been told that last night, there were three or four wolves in front of the lobby,' she is now telling us, 'so look after your little legs, girls!'

'Romania is full of stray dogs,' Benedetta murmurs. 'They say there are two or three hundred thousand. They must be dogs, not wolves.'

'Romania is the main European stronghold of wolves and bears,' Anna says. 'The presence of wolves is reported over an area of fifty-seven thousand square kilometres, and that of bears on fifty-two thousand square kilometres. The areas of distribution of the species cover twenty-five per cent of Romanian territory and are located especially in hilly and mountainous areas.'

We look at Anna like you would at some crazy person or a green alien. One, how does she know? Two, she has never said so many words in one go, let alone the word 'stronghold'. Three, so there really are wolves. Our mouths drop open, one by one.

'I looked it up on Wikipedia,' she whispers, and goes all red.

'You looked it up *and* memorized it,' says Carla. '*The areas of distribution of the species*? Who talks like that?'

'It also says they tear at their prey, starting from the belly. Because it's fattier,' Anna adds.

At the word 'tear', we all close our mouths, maybe because it's the opposite of what a wolf would do to a dead body. His mouth would open. He'd grab a hand. The arm. The face. Rachele tries to change the subject and starts explaining how the centralized system of Romanian sport works, and how the athletes live together all year round. She goes on about their dorms and bunk beds and discipline. I guess she'd be ready to list all their shampoos and menus too.

'Real discipline,' she says. 'Do you understand, children?'

She calls us children only once or twice a year. It's a treat. And here it is, the treat is being given to us today.

Some journalists come into the canteen, a clear sign that the most important day of this competition is really close. They take a few pictures, chat with the coaches, sneak a peek at Angelika. Then at Carla. I repeat 'Sunday Revolution and Wonder' and hope tomorrow one of them will need my photo too. I'll be sure to write my name down on a piece of paper, spelling it clearly, so both the Spanish and the Chinese press will be able to use it in the article about the Olympic hopefuls. My name will be on everyone's lips, on billboards, on the radio, and they'll be able to easily copy it from there. The M of Martina will be as big as the one at the mall.

'Martina,' says Carla, 'are you coming with us? Or do you want to keep stuffing yourself?'

I don't want to keep stuffing myself. I suddenly feel really fat, with the redhead's cellulite that can be seen through my tracksuit. My hair turns back to fire so I quickly get up and follow them. Rachele looks at me as if to say, 'Thank you' and I think, *You really are hopeless, Rachele. Stop smiling. Stop everything.* I must be thinking this with some force because she does stop smiling.

'Good girl,' Carla says when I stand up. 'Good and brave.'

Outside, the sunlight is bright on the snow, the sky dazzles, and the air smells incredible. I am good and I am brave. I am Martina with the biggest M in the world. I look back at the hotel and I see the bears with coats shovelling the snow, and they are still laughing. I like them, and their laughter, so I laugh too.

'You really are crazy,' Nadia says. 'But in a cute way.'

'Do you remember when Martina was little and she could only do left cartwheels?' Carla asks her. 'She used to say it was a question of order, whatever the hell that means.'

They have memories of me as a little girl, me and my left cartwheels, so I smile wider. I want to tell them that it didn't mean anything. It just seemed weird and terrible to start from the right. I tried to trick myself into it lots of times. Right cartwheels as a penance, right cartwheels as a challenge. In the end, after a whole year of trying, I managed to do them. Maybe now I'll get stuck again, just because they've mentioned it. I look up and see Karl watching us from a window. He waves, a large, exaggerated wave.

We run faster.

As we cross the bridge, we stop to watch the cars speeding along the A road below. We spit at them, we laugh, and we get to the sports centre in a great mood, despite all of our bruises. Despite all of our lives, hunger, and all of our pain. Outside the building there are birds and a few of the two or three hundred thousand stray dogs eating out of the rubbish bins.

'Gross,' says Carla. 'We should feed them the gymnast that has to die.'

'Aren't birds vegetarian?' I ask. But then I remember a documentary where an eagle was eating fish, snakes, and other birds.

'When I grow up, I want to know loads more things,' Nadia says, grabbing Carla's hand.

'Like what?' Carla looks at Nadia's hand. She smiles.

'How cities work. Or where the light comes from, through what pipes. How walls stay up. I'd like to know how you build bridges. All the things we take for granted. The hidden mechanisms. The mathematics of things.'

'The mathematics of things?' says Carla, laughing. 'Two and two is four. Ten plus ten is twenty.'

'Like what kind of mixture the pavement is made out of? Or our breath?' I say.

'Yes, that,' says Nadia. 'And stars. And water. And our hearts. Love.'

'And you want to know how babies are made, right?' Carla laughs.

'She wants to know how and when the wind changes direction,' I say. 'And what happens to your brain when you scream.'

'How darkness works,' Nadia adds. 'Or the void.'

'All that's on Google,' says Carla. 'Nothing special.'

She lets go of Nadia's hand. Light leaves Nadia's eyes.

'Aw,' says Nadia. 'You've ruined the magic.'

She has ruined the magic.

It's so early that the sports centre looks deserted. We walk down the corridors with their high ceilings and dim lights and we step into the first gym, which is still dark. The rings hang above our heads. Our steps echo in the stillness. As we cross it to get to our station, we hear the Chinese team in the second gym. It's dry. Quick. Terrible.

'Fucking dogs.' Carla clenches her jaw.

I know she's angry because she thinks she's different, but I know I'm angry because we are all the same. Romanians. Chinese. French. Italians. Girls of the world.

We move towards the noise and the shouting. I can also hear someone crying, so I look at Nadia and Carla. It is obvious they hear it too. My feet are made of wood, stone, glue. They are made of all the mistakes that got us here.

'Should we look?' Nadia whispers.

'I don't know,' I say. 'If they see us, they'll kill us.'

'It's more like if you see them, you'll kill yourself,' Carla says. 'They'll give you nightmares for a whole year.'

Carla and I look. I grit my teeth and immediately feel ill.

The shouts are coming from two girls and two boys. The face of their coach, standing before them, is dripping with sweat, thick lines – like cuts – on his forehead. This is what the face of someone who's about to die of a heart attack must look like. The face of that mythical coach Florin must have looked exactly the same. The face of Alex when his penis is hard is quite similar too.

Nadia pushes in between us, so we can all see. I squash myself against them, while the Chinese girls are caned on their backs and the boys are caned on their chests. I feel their pain. One body, one heart. One mega cane on all of our chests. One mega cane on all of our backs. I can feel it in my tummy but also where the cane lands and if the coach's face is that of someone about to die, then please let this be the moment for it to happen.

The coach manipulates them all into bridge positions, and starts kicking their feet and hands so they'll fall. And they do fall. Bridge, kick, fall. Bridge, kick, fall. We hear the sounds of broken breathing and choking, of lungs hitting the floor. I see their beautiful scores on the board during this past week. Then, the cane again.

'Why?' Nadia asks.

'They must have done something bad,' I say.

'Get real,' says Carla. 'This is how they always train. This is them being good athletes.'

The coach turns towards the door. His forehead is dripping and he is still shouting. The expressions on the faces of his gymnasts don't change despite the shouts, the falls, the cane. The coach's brain must be about to explode. He goes even redder while squeezing the arm of one of his athletes.

'This man has to die,' Carla says. 'They all have to die.'

Nadia looks at her and I know she has started seeing things. Now in her head the man is dead.

One of the boys falls to the floor. The coach runs towards him, so fast I think he's going to punch him. He gets him to do a handstand instead, and pushes him down as soon as he's up. Another handstand. Then, down again. He does it about twenty times, thirty maybe.

'How will they compete today?' I say.

'Maybe this is exactly what they think they need before competitions,' Carla says.

The boy looks at us. I close my eyes, hoping to disappear. Hoping to change the backdrop to my life and remove myself from here. But I open them again and the boy, in a handstand now, is still looking at us and I am not in Los Angeles nor in Bangkok. Eyes wide open, his back so very straight, right in front of me. Then he smiles the kind of smile you smile for the jury. Wide, perfect. And he smiles even more, until we run for it.

Gasping for air, we get to the main gym and take our tracksuits off. We stuff them in our bags and hide the bags under the chairs. When I get up, I see Carla kiss Nadia's eyes. She looks at me.

'Were you scared too, Martina? Do you need a kiss?'

I nod, so they hug me. And they kiss my eyes. I disentangle myself as soon as I can and start running around the gym. I can feel my breath bringing oxygen all the way to my knees, leaning into my chest, loosening my shoulders. I speed up, my heart speeds up too, and there is speed to my blood. Soon Carla and Nadia are running near me. We start jumping, stretching, and when Anna and Benedetta arrive, together with Alex and Rachele, we are already in a state of full concentration, right inside our own heads, good girls in their routine. No image of a raging Chinese coach can destroy us. And nothing can really touch us. We have warmed up, our backs are damp with sweat, adrenalin is already pumping. We have already erased all of what is evil from our drive. The lights come on with a loud click, the other teams take up their sections of the gym, and so the day begins.

'I love gymnastics,' Carla says. And we laugh because we really do. It's still our dream.

When Karl comes in, we're at the vault and the audience has already filled the arena for the Individual Finals, where the top gymnasts compete against each other for medals on each apparatus. Despite the busy stands, Carla must sense him coming in, with her shoulder blades maybe, because I'm standing right in front of her and see her face change. Nadia's face changes too but neither of them gives in and looks at him.

I do, because I can. He is sad. He is handsome, short and sad.

I watch him perform on the rings and his execution is faultless. His arms are straight and strong. I look at his hands and think back to him stroking Nadia and Carla's legs. It's very clear to me why you'd want to run off with him at night to see Romania-like-Paris and why it is difficult to stop wanting those hands, those eyes. I look at Carla, warming up at the bars now, fully focused for her day as a champion. She's quiet and Nadia, for the first time in years, seems to be in full control. Now that she has won Carla back, and Carla is no longer allowed to pronounce the letter K, she seems at peace. Her chin is pointing higher, and I'm sure that as of today her heart has a different shape too.

Maybe that of the moon.

Karl is watching them, Carla especially, with every chance he gets. I'm sure he doesn't understand what goes on between her and Nadia. And what exactly has expelled him from the system. How could he? How could he even begin to understand their one body and one heart, the blue pooh and their decision about the letter K? He cannot even begin to know that they have been sharing a bed since they were 4 years old, or about that abracadabra of theirs, which is so important to the whole team. He cannot begin to know that nothing can come between Nadia and Carla without being crushed. And if he doesn't know any of it, how could he possibly understand that Nadia has become the boss overnight? The one that sets the rules. The one to please and whose heart now has the shape of the moon. At any rate, looking carefully, Karl is not quite as handsome when he is sad, which is interesting in itself. His shoulders slump and his eyes slant downwards. I still hate Rachele for telling me 'Smile, Martina, you look prettier', but I understand her now, through the very easy example of the very sad face of the very sad Karl.

Carla is so sure of herself she convinces Rachele to let her add the *Produnova* at the vault. I imagine her ending up paralysed – still better than being a loser, according to her – but we have no time to picture her life in a wheelchair as she's already performing her jump so well it's like she has wings. The arena responds with sighs of wonder and a mega applause. In the crowd, the little girls that want to be us, here with their parents and friends, are all in awe. I was once one of those girls too.

'I love gymnastics,' Carla repeats. And we all repeat it too.

With her 15.6 on the vault, she is second only to Angelika, and conquers the silver podium. I look at them from eighth position, and try to feel proud of myself even here, where no medals are given but smiles are still needed. Eight is great for me, I tell myself. *I love this eight*, I repeat. And I love gymnastics.

Carla is then perfect at the bars, so precise and so fast she gets the third position on the podium. She smiles. She waves. Both her and Nadia perform a fantastic floor exercise. Their D scores are high, their execution is faultless. But Carla is second again and Nadia is third. Angelika, with her gymnastics that is beauty itself and magic itself, is always on the top step.

'Fuck that bitch,' I hear Carla say, looking at Angelika. 'I need her out of my life.'

She composes herself and goes with Nadia to the balance beam, confident and upbeat, possibly until the end of time, amen. But however well they perform on the beam, they don't beat Angelika. And their anger is so great that even if I do very well at the beam too and there is joy in my feet – and even if my shoulders and my hands are strong and my shape is elegant – nobody notices. There's no time to acknowledge me or any of the mediocrity of life. We quickly digest Benedetta's disappointing scores one after the other, and we try to just be glad that today, at the individuals, her presence doesn't affect the team. Today we compete for ourselves on every single apparatus and we win or we fail for ourselves in every single apparatus. As Carla holds back her tears on the podium when she receives her bronze medal, I find myself in fifth place at an international tournament for the first time in my life and for the first time since we arrived in Romania, Rachele gives me a genuine smile. I deserve a smile. I am strong. I too can be pretty. I am the pioneer of my present and my future.

After we are all done, we linger at the gym a bit more, to get all the other team's final scores. They appear on the board one after the other, one breath after the other.

'Whore,' Carla says, looking at Angelika winning her three gold medals and a silver. 'Whore, shithead, bitch.'

But we manage to celebrate Carla's two silvers and two bronzes anyway, and we manage to hug Nadia for her bronze at the bars. So as not to obsess about Angelika, we also decide to forever hate a few Chinese girls who stole our places on the podium and for the same reason we despise a Hungarian. I get a hug too, for my good score at the beam and my solid overall performance. The Useless Ones uselessly failed, but weren't as bad as the Spanish girls and that, for today and maybe in life, is just enough.

'I love you girls,' Rachele says. And we all say, 'We love you too.'

After lunch we go for an ice bath. There's no training in the afternoon, so that we won't be too tired tomorrow, for the All Around finals. Nadia and Carla get into the tub together, while I look at myself in the mirror. If today I nearly made it, will I be spectacular tomorrow? Or will I fail and will being fifth forever be the best I can do?

'Can you get into the ice if you have a period?' Nadia asks.

'Of course,' replies Carla. 'Blood might become ice, though!'

They mumble '*Brrr*,' launch a few swearwords in the air and sit down, gritting their teeth.

'China is stronger than ever,' Carla says.

By this stage in the game, all we can talk about is the competition. We evaluate, we estimate. We hate and we curse. We praise and we insult and we count and we wish. The way the scores are calculated has changed so many times that the maths has got complicated. So Nadia and Carla get into that.

'I need to get 14.70 on all the apparatus,' Carla adds. '14.90, for the glory.'

'I've got too much competition at the beam. And I am scared of getting stuck.'

'I need to crush the bitch. I can't fucking shake her off!'

'Khorkina: All Around world champion in 1997, 2001, and 2003. European champion in 1998, 2000, and 2002.' Nadia goes on reciting all of Khorkina's wins and scores as if numbers were a poem. A mantra. A rhyme.

'Why the fuck would you say that? What's with using a K?'

As I look at my face in the mirror, I notice a couple of spots and a few new lines under my eyes. I imagine myself older, making it to a hundred. I bite my lips, because Carla has told us it's an excellent way of plumping them up and making them look juicier. I bite and bite and my lips get juicier, smoother, and redder. It is a good trick. I plait my hair, while they rub ice over their heads and necks. The worst of the chill must have passed, if they're able to play with the cubes; the back is the part of your body that hurts the most in the ice. Then comes the head. Then comes the pleasure.

'What if I cut my hair?' I say.

I have never thought of it before. Or that I could ever cut my hair without my mum.

'Great idea!' exclaims Carla.

In one single second she gets out of the bath, ties a towel around her waist, and takes a pair of scissors from her make-up bag. Her nipples are pointy even without the Sellotape treatment. She sits me down on the toilet and Nadia watches us with a half-smile.

'How do you want it?'

'Short,' I say.

Carla chops off my plaits in one go. She smiles, so I smile too and look at my hair on the floor, still red, but no longer mine. And no longer on fire. It took me years to grow it long and I've decided to get rid of it in less than one minute. The broom my mum uses at the salon would sweep it up off the bathroom floor in a blink.

Carla carries on cutting and at this point there is nothing I can do. Nadia climbs out of the bath and asks if she can cut it too. She hates it when Carla touches someone else, and I can feel it.

'What do you say, Martina?'

'OK by me,' I reply.

'It's like a blood pact,' Nadia says. 'But with hair.'

Nadia grabs the scissors and takes over. Carla finishes putting lotion on her not-there tits, on her bruised legs, and on her bum. She brushes her hair, which now looks really long and precious, and every so often comes over to supervise. Nadia is cutting really slowly. I can feel the scissor tips caressing my skull, then the snip of metal and some very short hair falling on my shoulders.

It's gentle. I like it.

When they've finished they brush the hair from my neck with a make-up brush. They stand a step back to study me, tilting their heads, first to the right then to the left. I stare back at them, hoping to see a smile. But everything goes in slow motion as I watch them blink.

'So?' I ask.

Rachele will kill me, I think. Everyone will see the bald patches Carla and Nadia have left. I'll look like a crazy person and they'll probably upload photos of my crazy person's head online. Whatever I will do in my life, whatever backdrop of Vietnam or Laos I'll have behind me, people will know. They will remember. 'She's the crazy gymnast, see?' they'll say. I touch my nose twice but don't feel it under the tips of my fingers. The third time the nose is back there.

'You're beautiful,' Nadia says.

'Gorgeous,' Carla confirms. 'Like a superstar.'

I look at myself as Nadia runs her fingers through my bristly hair. I shiver as I spot no superstars in the mirror. I've never seen a girl with hair as short as mine and there is probably a reason for it. I touch it and it tickles against the palm of my hand, like the beige carpet at home scratches under my feet. I am not beautiful and my nose looks ten times bigger. I wish it really had disappeared, never mind searching for it with my fingers. I want to tell Mum, right away. I also want to tell her, 'Maybe if you cut all yours off too, you'll stop dreaming you have hair in your mouth.'

My eyes fill up with tears.

'Why are you crying? Have you changed your mind?' Carla asks.

'Not one bit. I love it.'

I hate it.

'And we love you,' says Nadia.

They probably hate me.

'So that's sorted,' confirms Carla. And once again we pretend that because someone says things are sorted, they really are sorted.

At seven we go for our physio session and I'm pleased to realize that my new hair makes me feel safer. Stronger. So I step into the battlefield with a new heartbeat. That of war. And, eventually, that of peace.

'What happened?' says Alex, looking at my shaved cranium.

I lie on my stomach. He gets the cream. My lungs close and the air in the room disappears. He squeezes the cream on his palms. The vastness of my pain is so enormous I can suddenly feel its power. With a scream I could break walls. With my agony I could make this whole hotel disintegrate and crumble. Then I would take care of the entire world.

'You want to talk about it?' Alex says.

'Shut up,' I say.

As I hear him massaging his hands, passing the white liquid from one to the other, I take a deep breath in, and shut down, I guess preparing for apnoea. In two seconds those hands will be on me. One second. I feel pressure building in my skull. My diaphragm clenching.

'Relax,' he says. 'It's all good.'

'Fuck this. Fuck you,' I say.

I stand up. I look at him, facing the monster full on. The room is moving. My head is spinning. I breathe out my terror and his terror, my pain and his horror, without lowering my eyes once.

'Fuck you!' I shout again.

'Martina,' he says.

I won't listen ever again. He can't say my name ever again. I walk away, I shut the door, and I shut my heart, with the certainty that he will never touch me again. If he does, I'll fucking kill him.

I go straight to the scheduled one-to-one meeting with Rachele. When we are staying in a hotel, each one of us is called to her room where she shifts the TV stand to make it look like an office desk. She puts a chair on each side and invites us in, saying, 'Come in. I'm so glad I get to see you alone for a few minutes.' But today, as I enter, she freezes. Her script fails her. Her smile vanishes as she gets up off the chair.

'What have you done to your hair?'

'Trimmed it?'

'Martina, it's *butchered*, not trimmed. Was it Carla?'
'It was me.'

She remains silent for a few seconds. I don't understand if she feels sorry for me or if she's about to get angry and shout at me. Whatever will follow, I can take it. Whatever will follow, my agony will pulverize it, so the doubt doesn't bother me much. I see the Chinese coach's cane, and imagine him giving it to Rachele to beat me. Then me beating her. I focus on her cheesy thighs and hope she's not going to cry. Emotions are the worst.

'I feel better with my hair short,' I say.

As she still isn't saying anything, I repeat myself, louder.

'I feel better with my hair short. And I feel stronger.'

Strong is the right word to use with her. Even though I might have done something stupid, tomorrow I have my most important competition to date, and if shaving my hair off makes me feel stronger, then she has to support me. She can tell me off on Monday. She will also be able to tell me I am stupid and dumb and horrible. But now she has to say that I really do seem stronger and that she believes in me.

She looks at me closely. She gets up and studies the hair at the back of my head.

'It looks terrible from behind. Like someone ate your hair.'

She rummages around in the bathroom then comes back with a pair of nail scissors. I think about her toenails, hard and a little yellowed. I think about her skin when she hugs me, the smell it leaves. She wets my head with water from the tap and tidies up my haircut as best she can.

'It's true you look strong, Martina.'
'I feel it. I also feel safer.'

She pauses. We both know what I mean. But once again she decides not to hear me. Or to say anything out loud. Suddenly I wonder if she had in fact gone to the higher floors, and she had told everything about Alex, and she too was waiting for something to happen. Maybe she even went to the police but the police were for some obscure reason on Alex's side. Reasons like those you find on Twitter, of secret paedo gangs going up to all the places of power and the FBI and the Vatican and the White House being part of it all.

'Strong and safe is good,' she murmurs. 'It's great, actually. You must remember it tomorrow. And remember that you can succeed at anything if you really want it.'

I listen to her and know she will repeat this same sentence to the team until eight o'clock this evening. I know that she too has gone back to her script and wants to help us sleep, compete, be serene. Win. I also know that at the end of the day she will cry and eat too much chocolate and drink too much vodka and, after all, she has never been a champion herself, and she has failed in everything herself, so all these words have not worked for her.

'Have Carla and Nadia been nice to you this week?'

'Of course. So nice.'

'Why did they fall out?'

'I really don't know.'

'Did you see them make up?'

'No.'

'Do you mind talking about it?'

'It's boring.'

Rachele swallows my rebuff as I run my hands over my strong-girl hair.

Tomorrow is Sunday, and Sunday is the first day of Revolution and Wonder. I will be clean and precise in the exercises. I will not fall off the balancing beam or be scared. I will grab the bars with strength and I will execute faultless twists, and holds, and jumps. At the end of my perfect routine, I will smile and shed a single tear while running my hand over my super short hair. Over my super strong skull. The gesture, the caress over my skull, my head leaning back a little and my eyes looking up at the neon lights, will become my new abracadabra. And my signature pose. I've been looking for one for ages.

When we were little, we did competitions on mats arranged lengthwise. In a row, one after the other. The floor exercise didn't include diagonals. We spent our Sundays in our leotards and our plimsolls, snacking on fizzy drinks and crisps. There were always vending machines in the gyms and we liked them a lot, even if back then too we were forbidden from putting on weight. Sometimes my mum came and sometimes she worked or slept instead. When my dad came I didn't look at him like some other girls looked at their dads before a competition. Carla's parents always came and Nadia's parents, actually her one parent, her mum, practically never did. Nadia used to say her mum was happy that competitions were on Sundays because she could have at least one complete day of the week not being a mum. On Sundays she'd have her girlfriends round, or go for a motorbike ride with her gang and do fun stuff, which since she had Nadia the mistake very young, and Nadia was still small, she could hardly ever do. This taught us that it's not necessarily nice being a mum and it is possible to wish to be as away as possible from your children. But it also taught us that some mums have a gang of friends and ride on motorbikes, drink beer, and really laugh.

There was one time when Nadia's mum came to watch us and Nadia didn't perform as well as usual. She was getting over tendonitis of her left foot. In the previous few months we had trained hard and each one of us had reacted to the punishments our bodies took in different ways. Benedetta and Anna, for example, had started taking laxatives to lose weight. Carla had experienced her first twisties – she had lost her bearings while turning in the air – which left us terrified. Caterina had suffered all those fractures and had abandoned the team. I had started doing things twice, and so on.

Nadia's mum had been impressed all the same because it had been ages since she'd watched her daughter do gymnastics. I don't think she actually knew what doing gymnastics meant and involved. She hadn't realized how good Nadia had got and how complicated her skills had become. She came into the changing room while we were showering, congratulated us, and while I worked shampoo into my hair, I saw tears of happiness pouring down Nadia's cheeks. Or maybe it was just the shower.

'You're all so tiny,' her mum said, peering at us under the jets of water. 'And so cute!'

She said it as if she'd just seen some little puppies. Nadia got dressed and smiled because it really was a lovely Sunday and she was so tiny and so cute. She was also good and got lots of compliments. Her tendonitis was getting better and now that her mum had seen her, it'd all been worth it. Carla nestled on Nadia's mum's lap to have her hair brushed and Nadia brushed her own. I felt jealous for her. Her mum was very beautiful and I would have liked to nestle in her arms too. She had been so lovely that I'd hoped for weeks that she would come back. But she never did.

Before dinner we call home. To be precise, three texts are sent from our three beds at the same time to our mums or dads and a few seconds later our phones ring, each with their own ring tone. Mine is embarrassing, the tune of a Mickey Mouse cartoon I used to watch when I was maybe 8 and that I'm now too superstitious to change.

'It's raining here,' Dad says.

'Here it's snowing.'

'How are you?'

'I like Romania. I'm good.'

'Have you been on any other outings since the mall?'

'We've been busy training.'

'We're treating ourselves tonight and going to the cinema.'

I know he is lying but I don't want to ruin the lie for them. I breathe in. And out. He'll have to come up with a fake plot and a fake review for the fake movie.

'Tomorrow,' he says. 'Revolution and Wonder!'

'Do you think I've already been to Romania in a previous life?' I ask him. 'I feel good here.'

'We'll have to check the cards,' he laughs. 'But my gut feeling is yes, big time.'

'I thought so. We'll watch the videos together when I'm back, OK?'

We used to spend entire evenings at home, and sometimes entire afternoons at the gym, watching videos of the competitions. Whenever I watch myself, I'm again afraid of falling over, as if I don't already know the outcome. I picture myself crashing down on my neck and being taken away on a stretcher.

'Look at those chubby legs,' Carla would say when she rewatched herself. 'When we're done with gymnastics, let's go straight to get ourselves fixed!'

'Can we be stretched taller?' Nadia would ask.

'And we can have cameras filming us as our height and width are modified. But it's too late to do something about osteoporosis.'

'We'd get that anyway by the time we're fifty. So what's the difference in having it done at fourteen?'

Since the very beginning, when Carla trained or when some exercise didn't come off the way she wanted, she was always the most diligent in the whole gym. She didn't talk, she kept her head down, her jaw clenched. She was able to repeat her routine more times than all of us, like she was not allowed to leave that Tuesday, that Wednesday, without having given her best and without having found a solution to the problem. And the next day, she'd never feel tired, despite the effort she'd made. She started all over again, rested, attentive. Her head bowed down, abs tensed, eyes focused.

'Good girl,' Rachele and all the other coaches always told her. And Carla would nod.

She knew she was a good girl.

Tonight we have such an early dinner, it isn't even dark outside. Rachele gives us a team speech and for a second I am worried she will say 'Amen' at the end of it. She doesn't, thank God, and pours herself a beer. I see her raise a glass to a few other coaches. Some smile back but they all probably think she's pathetic. Alex is telling another physiotherapist something he's read about. 'Overtraining,' I think I hear as I watch the judges sit at a table by themselves. Do some of them exchange our naked pictures? How many of them are good and how many are bad?

'Anna, do you see how beautiful Martina has become?' Carla says.

Anna looks me in the eyes to work out if I've been punished or if I'm happy with my haircut.

'It would be even more dramatic if you did it,' Carla tells her. 'Shear off all that wool!'

'I'll think about it,' Anna mumbles.

While Benedetta is pretending to read Anna's palm and predict her future, Karl comes in and walks towards our table. I look down and watch his legs until he is right next to me. Nadia and Carla are staring at the void near him, making him instantly invisible. A moment ago, he had a body, now he is a ghost. Abracadabra.

'There's a terrible smell,' Carla says. 'Of people from underprivileged countries.'

When she says 'underprivileged' she rolls her eyes, to stress her aversion. Someone should stop her. And fight the evil and the bad she brings in. But we don't. We comply even when we hate it. Even when we know it's wrong and disgusting. That's how most evil things of life work. They slip in without finding any resistance.

'Yes, and of dwarfs,' Nadia adds.

'I can smell poverty, dwarfs, and pimples,' Carla continues.

'I can smell poverty dwarfs, pimples, and losers.'

'And too much wanking,' she finishes under her breath.

I don't know how much Karl can understand. But even if he doesn't speak or understand our language, Nadia and Carla's tone of voice is so cruel that his knees swivel and he moves away. The words keep going round and round in my head too. They are like glue and have such sticky filaments they won't budge from behind my forehead and the back of my eyes. All I can now see is a pimply dwarf in a poor room wanking after losing a competition. Such is the power of Carla's voice.

'Down with the letter K!' Carla says.

'Down with the letter K!' Nadia echoes.

That evening we tidy up our room and throw away the cans of Fanta and Coca-Cola, our notes, the trash. We fold some of our clothes. We check our hair in the bikini area and under our armpits. Nadia rewatches the Chinese training session, which she secretly filmed while Carla gave us a test on phobias. She asks: *Do you believe that if you perform specific actions (like counting, checking, engaging in ritual behaviour to ward off bad luck, etc.) you will be able to change your destiny?* and something inside me dies a little. I do believe that by counting I can change my destiny. It turns out Nadia and I score between seventy-seven and ninety-eight points, which isn't good.

'Too bad.' Nadia smiles.

We hang up our pink competition leotards and worship them as if they are our gods. We kneel in front of them, laughing, and we pray to the snow and to the cold, to Romania, and to our motherland, and we promise our souls to the devil, to Khorkina despite the letter K, to Nadia Comaneci, and whoever the hell may want them, in exchange for a crushing victory.

'To win, to win, to win,' we whisper.

'Come on, come on, come on!' we shout.

Carla goes to the bathroom and Nadia and I go back to the window to see if we can spot a lucky wolf. Or Angelika, which is kind of the same. Down there the bear father and the bear son in their coats are shovelling the snow.

'Thank you, Martina.'

'What for?'

'For not spilling the beans to anyone,' Nadia says. 'For protecting me, Carla, and our secrets.'

'I wouldn't have known what to spill anyway.'

And Nadia, grateful and soft, tells me that she loves Carla and Carla wanted to kiss Karl and they'd all started touching each other and then Carla stopped touching her and couldn't take her hands off Karl. Nadia was so jealous she wanted to die.

'That idiot Karl. I hope he is the one actually dying,' she says.

We really hope way too many people will die, I think.

Nadia explains she's never really fancied him, she just pretended she found him handsome – well, she says he really is handsome but who cares? She did it to provoke Carla. To bring her closer. To bring her only love closer. But things got out of control.

'Now everything is OK.' She turns to me and runs her hand over my head. 'Carla loves only me and there are no wolves and no Karls out there.'

She walks over to the bathroom and goes in to see her only love. I quickly take my clothes off and slip into my T-shirt for the night, taking advantage of the fact that I'm on my own and there's no one staring at my growing cellulite and my dwarf's hips. I lie on the bed and switch off the ceiling light. Through the window I can see at least a million stars and I hope I'll find my only love too. I hope our love will be glorious. And together we will walk all the streets and roads and paths of the world.

'I'm scared,' I hear Carla say in the middle of the night.

I've never heard Carla say she's scared. But I must not obsess over it. If Carla and Nadia can't sleep even the night before our most important competition, fine. But I know my legs will turn to jelly and my hands will go all tingly. I *must* sleep. I *must* do well tomorrow. It's my great chance to be noticed. To do even better than today. To aim for the Olympics.

'Don't be scared,' says Nadia. 'I'll protect you forever.'

'If only that fat dirty revolting girl had died tonight. Then first place would be mine.'

Another one we want dead, see? I've lost count.

'Don't worry,' Nadia says. 'You've got this.'

'Yes, but if she wasn't here everything would be easier. For me and for the team.'

'You'll win anyway.'

'You don't know that.'

'I do. You are a superstar.'

'Remember just one thing,' Carla says. 'If tomorrow you go over 60 you must take your clothes off. In front of everyone.'

They giggle.

'Getting to 60 would be like liquid gold.'

'We'll all see you naked and that will be like liquid gold.'

They start laughing loudly and say silly things about liquid gold and how it must feel to have liquid gold poured over your head and down your back. They repeat it so many times I end up picturing it too. I can feel hot shiny gold wax running down my spine, through my legs, to my feet. It feels great, it feels magic. Most of all, it feels healing. So I fall asleep at peace, ready to greet the Sunday of Revolution and Wonder, all covered in magic and liquid gold and not, as it would turn out, in blood.

SUNDAY

Revolution and Wonder

'Look at her,' says Carla.

I stretch my arms and see the whitest sky. It's like a sheet of paper and I want to reach out and write *Today is the day of Revolution and Wonder* across it.

'Martina, get up and come and look at her.'

Carla presses her face against the window so I do the same. As our noses are squashed against the glass and our eyes are still sleepy, I imagine someone taking our photo from inside the woods. The hotel in the snow, the atmosphere of competition. Our room seen from outside. Our eyes seen from outside. The anticipation they carry. The fear.

'What?'

'Can't you see her?'

When the last bit of this competition is done and the All Around scores are totted up, the best of us, along with very few of the best losers, will get to *book a ticket* to the next country, the next qualifiers, then finally, the Olympics. We always say 'book a ticket' and I hate the expression, it sounds like we've won a prize holiday to somewhere warm that will have a tropical buffet and piña coladas when in fact we are killing ourselves with hard work. With sweat and anger and pain.

'She's been like that for over six minutes,' Carla says.

I expect to see Angelika but I look closer and I see Nadia is doing a handstand at the edge of the forest, risking strain and cold. She knows very well we can see her from here. And she knows very well she shouldn't be out there alone. Her puffer jacket has fallen down over her face but we recognize her feet, her tracksuit and her being Nadia in every bit of her body. She's wet and dirty. There is mud on her.

'Why is she doing that?' Carla says.

I shrug and run a hand over my prickly new hair. Maybe Mum will never dream of hair in her mouth again, because as of today, the Sunday of Revolution and Wonder, certain threads and memories, fingers and horrors, are destined to disappear not only from my head but from her mind too.

'If she gets sick before we crush the other clubs, she really is an idiot,' Carla says. 'She was out all night.'

'Was she?' I ask.

You can see all the way from here that Nadia is shaking. She comes off the handstand, looks at us and smiles, waving her hand. She runs towards the hotel and I lie back on the bed. I feel very tired, as if I haven't slept for a single minute. Or ever in my life. All the words and the wolves in the forest and these two tossing and turning in their beds and leaving in the middle of the night have left me exhausted. I look at Carla and she is shaking too.

'Everything OK?' I ask. 'You look pale.'

'Let's just be silent,' she replies.

It is OK by me, so we stop talking. Nadia comes back, drops her very dirty jacket, goes straight into the bathroom, and turns on the shower. She stays in there forever. When she gets out, she is very quiet and we embrace that quietness, the focus that we need. We do our hair – mine takes zero seconds – and make-up in silence. Carla puts eye shadow on both of us and they add eyeliner. I don't because it makes everything blurry.

'What's wrong?' she asks Nadia.

'All good,' she says.

But she keeps on scratching her hand. Then her arm.

We slip on our way-too-pink-with-way-too-many-sequins leotards. We stick them with the spray glue on our skin, we prepare our bags, drink some water, and brush our teeth. We also wash our feet with great care, especially the soles, which today of all days should not be dirty.

'Off we go,' Carla says.

And off we go.

Rachele is waiting for us in the hotel conference room for what she calls our 'visual training session'. The room is almost dark and in the dark it seems less drab. At 'visual training' we are not even allowed to say 'hi', so we don't say it. We just go in and take our places on the floor.

I sit next to Anna and Benedetta, and together with Carla and Nadia we all cross our legs. Alex looks at us. I wish we could all look at him in the same second and as one body, one heart, judge him so hard his heart will break, then he'll fall to his knees and ask to be forgiven.

We wouldn't forgive him.

We all look down, sitting in this circle of love and trust, and do some slow breathing before Rachele starts her speech. I open and close my fleece twice, while we mimic our intent faces. We know it's what is expected from us and from our faces. Deep focus. So deep focus we deliver. We listen to her as she talks us into a state of relaxation, making us visualize a place that is clean and silent, pure and safe, while we climb the seven steps to concentration, so our minds will lead our bodies. It smells like pee in here, and I wonder if I have actually been smelling it all the time I've been away from home. Or since the very beginning of my life.

'Your body is your mind,' Rachele says. 'Your body is the team's body.'

We stay silent. We are too close to the competition to say stuff that doesn't have anything to do with it and even stuff that does have something to do with it. When I peek at them, Alex and Rachele have their most serious faces on, furrowed and severe. Sometimes I sort of remember that the two of them work for us – and it's not the other way around – and this makes me feel like I have some sort of power. And control. I know I don't, but it's an easy way out of pain.

I count, breathe in and out, and start visualizing the warm-up. I visualize the gym as Rachele is telling me to do, well lit and empty of people.

'The audience doesn't exist,' she whispers. 'Gravity doesn't exist.'

And the audience doesn't exist and gravity doesn't exist. The stands are empty. I feel light, strong, and I am able to perform the exercises faultlessly. I place my feet, hold in my tummy, straighten my legs. I jump, I fly, and I conquer all beauty and all magic. The vault is a trampoline able to make you cover the distance to the other planets. The beam is a line, nothing under it, where it's impossible to fall and get hurt. Then I land. My heart is beating a regular rhythm and the spotlights are shining only for me.

'The warmth you are feeling on your face, on your body, is the light of victory,' Rachele says.

In the light of victory I get distracted, because I see myself with long hair and I have to readjust the image halfway through a handspring. I open one eye and see Carla look at Nadia. She looks at me too, scared, and immediately closes her eyes.

'You are ready, girls,' Rachele finishes. 'And you are the best.'

When we, the best, are done with the visualization we leave the conference room and walk to the canteen. My tummy is relaxed, all my muscles are relaxed, and I feel good. I look over at my teammates and hope they all feel like I do. Good, relaxed, and focused. I hope that Nadia isn't too anxious, and Anna will be sure-footed in the double somersault on the last diagonal. I hope Benedetta isn't too desperate about not being able to compete today or too angry that she had to warm up anyway: it's the rule and you don't discuss the rules. I hope Carla crushes Angelika and that we will all get to fly on more planes, sleep in new places, and win, always. I hope I'll put in a great performance, the best one of my life, and I hope they notice me. I hope I make it to the top sixteen gymnasts of this tournament. Better, to the top ten. And all the coaches and the national team's technical director will come and tell me I'm good.

I also really hope I don't die.

'You are one heart,' Rachele says once more when we get to the canteen, 'and I love your heart.'

Her voice is annoying me now. It gets creepy, especially when she wants us to feel emotional and pretends to love us. It's a bit like when Mum starts explaining to me why people are sad or why people are happy and her tone is a cross between storytelling and fake sweetness. She gives me the shivers, with those eyes of hers when they try to *communicate*. We all know by now that it isn't her biggest strength.

'Even when you compete against each other, you are one body, take care of it,' says Rachele.

'And you are one mind, take care of it,' Alex concludes as we sit down.

With our shared mind, we knock him down. Carla burps, a burp which fills the room, flying over the other tables, our heads, and the whole Sunday. Here comes her body. Here comes her gut. We laugh, forget about the seven steps, the concentration, and we start our breakfast. Rachele drinks her coffee and finally stops talking.

Wrapped up in our puffer jackets, our heads in our hats, we cross the forecourt, then go over the bridge and cross the A road. I turn around and look at the other teams walking in the snow behind us. I see the Russians and spot the Hungarians. I see the Chinese club.

Sometimes I still believe this is not only my life, but also my most-hoped-for dream. Like now, when I'm walking towards the vault, the podium, the mat, the beam. All I have to do is compete and there's nothing I want more. I'm about to perform a floor exercise that has cost me years of deprivation, mornings of training, afternoons of preparation, strict diets, and hand cramps and back pain. Bone pain. Pills. But I am not scared and I am not sad. I feel great, I feel like a warrior, and maybe it really is the Sunday of Revolution and Wonder.

'Karl,' Carla whispers.

The Polish team is at the other end of the bridge. Karl is walking in front of us, alone, and he doesn't turn. Looking at Carla's face, you'd think the word Karl had come out by accident. Like the burp in the canteen. In fact, she doesn't say it again or add anything. I stick my earphones in and crank up my old iPod and picture the same scene with a soundtrack. I replay the same scene with a soundtrack and myself as the romantic lead. I am the girl Karl is thinking about, we are in love, walking in the snow, in a foreign country of mountains and villages with medieval buildings.

We say 'I love you'. We kiss. We know how to fly.

At the arena each club sits under their own flag. The lights are very bright. Too bright. Not exactly like I had visualized in the conference room. The names and countries of the athletes competing at the All Around are announced through the loudspeakers to background tracks of the chosen floor music. The stands are crowded and from down here, the people look like confetti, the noise like a buzz of a giant mosquito about to bite us. The smell is a mixture of floor soap and sweat. Their sweat. My sweat.

We take up our positions on our team bench, not too far from the Chinese and the Spanish. I pull my zip up and down twice and pick up and put down my water bottle twice. The judges are milling about in the jury area, while Rachele is talking to Alex. He is massaging Anna's sore ankle.

'Better?' he is asking her.

And as usual she is only capable of nodding and holding back her tears. I imagine going to the microphone and saying out loud, *How many of you guys are being touched by your physios? What about your coaches? How many of you want to stop being alive and can't breathe at night?* Shall we be the pioneers of that more than anything, the pioneers of our dreams and of our freedom, and still jump and fly between uneven bars – between one galaxy and the other – but without any of the adults making up the rules?

In the far corner of the arena, Nadia is peering at the uneven bars as if they're a mathematical formula she needs to solve. She is so pale it's like the blood has left her body forever. I look at the French girls, I look at the Spanish girls, and I look for a way out. I look for the Romanian girls but they aren't here yet. Anna lies down on her back. She has made it here, despite being a Useless One. She should be proud.

'Are you proud?' I ask her.

'Not really. And I need to relax. I'm not focused yet.'

'I'm not OK yet either,' I say. 'Something is off today.'

She looks as if her eyesight has gone fuzzy, like short sighted people peer in photographs. We are one body, one heart, so I turn away from her blurry eyesight. I don't want to get infected by her virus of blurriness. From where I stand, the Polish girls look like they're going to be today's losers. I can see their anxiety from here and in their grey, terrified faces. I don't know if I should tell Rachele, explain how obvious it is that they are going to lose. Or better yet, say nothing because it might bring bad luck.

Better say nothing.

'Red red yellow blue – Coca-Cola Fanta glue – teeth straight feet straight – me me but it's you – blue pooh Fanta glue – I protect and so do you,' Carla and Nadia are reciting. They then take turns to run their hands over my bristly hair. If the competition goes well today my skull will become a fixed part of the spell. I risk having to carry these caresses with me for years.

'Have you tried abracadabra instead?' I hiss.

'What's up with you?' Nadia asks me. 'Are you angry?'

Her hands are covered in scratches. What's up with *me*?

'Look at how she's working her jaw. She's nervous, that's what,' sneers Carla. 'Marti at the All Around is a big deal!'

They walk away and I touch my jaw. I am not *working* my jaw. What an expression anyway. Why would Carla say that? Immediately, my face feels like a camel's, my mouth moving sideways, my teeth sticking out. Working it. I strip down to my leotard and on cue, Alex comes over and starts rubbing my legs, my arms. He also gives me a hand massage, pulling on each finger, and with a cloth he wipes off the leftover lotion.

'We don't want to slip, do we?' he says. Then, 'Shall we make peace?'

I see myself slipping from the higher bar and I have to chase away the sound of my neck breaking. I then see myself breaking his neck.

'Fuck off,' I tell him.

I stand up. Leave. The Romanian club arrive and the girls are the most beautiful of all of us. I mean, each one of them is prettier than each one of us and than all the other teams in the universe. Even their lactic acid and their muscles are probably better. And their blood. They have glitter in their hair, shiny red leotards, and blue eyeliner tipping upwards on their eyelids. I watch them and in my mind I imagine them performing in slow motion, ponytails swinging and bandaged feet stepping lightly on the lino floor, as flexible as caterpillars. The bandages on their wrists look like precious bracelets, their legs are longer than ours, their hips narrower. I choose a soundtrack to highlight their superiority, classical music will do, it makes everything even more striking. I look for Angelika Ladeci, the star of my own slow-mo movie, but she isn't there.

'Angelika?' comes a murmur from all sides.

'Ladeci?' we hear.

'Ladeci?' we say.

Maybe she wants to make a special entrance and arrive after everyone else, so we'll all watch her, the protagonist. Or maybe she wants us to worry, so we'll love her even more. But the Romanian coach's eyes are panicky, their upward-pointing eyeliner failing to hide their terror.

'Angelika's missing,' Carla whispers. 'What the *fuck*?'

Nadia grabs her arm, ecstatic, as she recites their rhyme again. I look at Rachele, her hand over her mouth, the other in a tight fist. Anna and Benedetta are standing next to her and they all look terrified. We sit close together and watch the Romanian coach approach the jury. Only Carla looks relieved.

'Maybe they trained her too hard and her body has broken,' Anna says.

That has happened before. Something in the body of a gymnast broke suddenly, and she couldn't compete at the last minute. Or ever again. Or maybe Angelika has run away out of despair. Maybe she's had enough of faking her perfect smile. Of winning gold medals that stink of men. She has *booked her ticket* but for out of here.

Lucky her.

Rachele exchanges looks with the other coaches and they walk up to the jury in a group. The LED numbers are blinking quickly, too quickly, so I figure that the scoreboard technician has disappeared too. Maybe he is with Angelika and everyone else who has decided, this Sunday morning, to restart their lives elsewhere. I see them all walking free, feet sinking in the snow, towards an easier place where they won't be constantly watched and constantly judged and yelled at, and where no one is cruel. Maybe this is the Revolution my dad was talking about. Maybe this is the Wonder. Today is the day when we free ourselves from constriction, routine, and the fear of falling and dying with a broken neck. From the claustrophobia we get from push-ups in sets of thirty and another thirty and another thirty and another thirty. From this Sunday onwards, winning in a gym will no longer be important and bowing with a smile will no longer be needed.

At the jury's station, the coaches are getting worked up, moving their hands, frowning. I can't hear them. I think about their lives, which might even be more skewed than ours. Where are their families? Why are they so sick? Am I going to turn into them? We've had several coaches, at our local clubs and then at the national squad. At the beginning we would always look up to them. Love them, even. Slowly we would fight with them and they would made us cry, often just because they wanted to. They intended to upset us. To enslave us. Make us feel weak and useless. By then, we would only fear them and stick to fear as the key sentiment to make us move forward. And better. But now I know from watching Rachele and Alex, from looking at the monster in the eyes, that they cry too and they are lonely too; they are liars, weak, evil, and worst of all, they are failed gymnasts. They have no talent whatsoever. Fear is leaving space for something new, which is only ours. And is our true weapon. Hate.

The first coach we had at the Team Training Camp, Vittorio, used to give us lessons on our possible future path in life, letting us know that staying had a price and a meaning bigger than ourselves. And our happiness. Once, I must have been 7 or 8, he explained that training a gymnast is like holding a sparrow in your hand.

'If you hold too tight, it dies. If you don't hold tight enough, it flies away,' he said.

At home I repeated the sparrow metaphor. I found it poetic and something to be proud of. To be a sparrow in someone else's hands, what delight. Vittorio said it many more times and used to repeat it when he pushed us over our limits. And just like that, 'sparrow' stopped sounding like a lovely word, and being in someone's hands ceased to be something to be happy about.

'In gymnastics you need a pianist's precision of execution and the muscular effort of a weightlifter,' he would say. 'They are opposite skills, which should be trained in different ways. The pianist must practise daily and at length. The weightlifter, by contrast, only occasionally needs to exert maximum effort and needs a lot of rest. But if a pianist makes a mistake nothing happens, while if a gymnast makes a mistake she can die.'

I saw myself and a million sparrows die.

'It's like dissolving salt in water,' Vittorio said, before leaving us and gymnasts forever. 'You are trying to add more and more. At first, it's easy, then it gets more difficult. You need to stir harder, longer. Maybe with water you can make a science of these things. But in training there is no magic formula. It doesn't take much to overdo it. It doesn't take much to get an oversaturated solution.'

'What does oversaturated even mean?' Carla had asked.

It was one of the first times I had seen her train. We

were all kids. And even with no magic formula, no rhymes, and no Bible, she was already magic.

'Whatever it means, it doesn't sound too good,' Nadia had told her.

At some level, all gymnasts are oversaturated solutions and maybe Angelika had become oversaturated. I picture her in a glass full of water and salt, and in that glass there is no air to breathe, nothing to be happy about. We are in there too. So is the Chinese team. Together with all of those who are in this room sporting Lycra leotards and deformed muscles. Oversaturated solutions and bruised bodies floating in glasses of water and salt.

Rachele comes towards us and whispers something in Alex's ear, who in turn whispers something in her ear. It is like a game of Chinese whispers and I know it will fall to me to try to make out the meaningless sentence and say it out loud. Rachele looks over at the other coaches whispering in the other physiotherapists' ears. They are all standing, and it's clear this is an emergency.

She turns to us.

'Angelika Ladeci has gone missing,' she says.

'*Missing?*' I say. 'Since when?'

'Last night. This morning. They don't know.'

'They don't *know?*' Carla asks. 'Has she gone home because she can't stand the threat of me?'

'They saw her go to bed but they don't know if she went missing during the night or this morning.'

'Idiots,' Carla says. 'They make out they're so strict, punching their athletes in the guts, and then they go and lose Angelika.'

'So what happens now?' Anna asks.

'Now the competition happens,' says Rachele. 'Obviously the Romanians want it stopped while they look for her.'

161

And here she makes a circle above her head to indicate the crowded terraces, the bright lights, the polished apparatuses, the teams who have started warming up. 'But do you think an event like this can be stopped? Plus, we've all got flights back. If they can't look after their champion, why should we all pay the price?'

'What could have happened?' Benedetta asks.

'Broken record. How about moving our well-trained backsides?' Carla suggests. 'Benedetta, next time you decide to speak, warn us, because it's always a shock to be reminded you have a voice.'

Carla gets up, pinches Benedetta's bum cheek, and takes off her tracksuit. She runs her hands through her blonde ponytail and stretches her fingers and her shoulders before rubbing her ankles. She touches the callouses on her hands to check they are all still there. They are. It would be enough for one of them to come off to make the exercises painful.

'She's finally out of here,' Nadia says.

'Maybe she's got diarrhoea and is too embarrassed to say anything,' says Carla.

She winks and bursts out laughing. She puts her index finger in front of her mouth and with her eyes seems to also be saying *don't overdo it, come on*. Nadia strips down to her leotard, fixes it, and thanks to the shiny sequins, and thanks to their smiles, the competition begins. I caress my cropped hair, adjust my pink leotard too, and try to concentrate, with my earphones in. I stretch, rub my hands and feet, peeking every so often at the other teams. I close my eyes, think of my mum and dad. Of their few real smiles. Of their few real hugs. I reopen them and see snow outside the window, flakes like flying saucers. I'd really like to taste them. To catch a few on my tongue and crunch them like crackers. It's my first All Around at such an important competition and I still can't believe it.

'You are the best,' I say to myself. 'You are a warrior and a pioneer.'

The five of us walk in formation to the vault. Benedetta is with us because even if she is not competing, we are still a team and we are still one body. We cannot walk without her two legs. The other competitors are everywhere, behind us and in front of us. The Romanians, who look worried, and the Chinese – whose expressions mirror ours, efficient robots who won't rebel – the French, who can all aspire to be models but currently all suck at gymnastics, and the Polish, who look like they had food poisoning about two hours ago. Each one of us today will compete against one another on all the apparatuses, and at the end of the day there will only be one podium, three rankings on the most coveted one of this competition.

One and only one gold medal.

The soundtracks for the floor routines start by the mats and every so often I hear a tune repeated because a Spanish athlete has chosen the same one as a Russian and an English athlete has the same preference as a French one. I bite my tongue twice, very gently, and twice again a little harder.

'Pioneer,' I repeat.

Even though, I am not sure why, in my mind the word becomes musketeer. Behind us, a French competitor approaches the uneven bars. Her sounds on the bars suddenly remind me of when my mum's hoover bangs against the stairs as she cleans, then the sound of my forehead moving up and down on the physio bed.

'You are a warrior,' I repeat to myself. 'But a nice one that fights for peace. Nothing bad can happen to those who are good.'

'Red red yellow blue – Coca-Cola Fanta glue – teeth straight feet straight – me me but it's you – blue pooh Fanta glue – I protect and so do you,' Nadia and Carla say before moving apart.

And by then all things are in fast forward, the bodies, the thoughts, the words, the jumps, the falls, and I am already running towards the springboard, rotating my hands, bouncing in the air, double twisting – then nailing a *Yurchenko* and landing without problems, without shifting my feet by one single millimetre.

I bow to the jury. I bow to the audience.

I wait for my score, and welcome a good 14.4, as I watch a perfect Chinese gymnast jump after me, then land planting herself on the ground without moving a single muscle, not even an eyebrow. Maybe not even a heartbeat. There comes her 14.8. She is followed by a French, then a Spanish girl I will not see again because she isn't good enough, and because her team isn't as strong as mine, or the Romanians and the Russians, let alone the Chinese.

I move on to the balance beam. I perform my routine as if I'm still in Rachele's guided meditation. All is clear. All is easy. Gravity doesn't exist. Pain doesn't exist. I jump. I land.

I bow to the jury. I bow to the audience.

To the world.

As the morning goes by, Carla – accompanied by the soundtrack of feet landing, of bodies thudding or falling, of numbers spinning on scoreboards, and polite or wild applause from the audience – is carving her name on everyone's mind. After her incredible 15.183 at the vault, and a 14.86 at the beam, she receives a great 14.8 at the bars. When she smiles, her smile is the sweetest ever. When she jumps, she jumps like no one else in the arena and when she dances, her moves are so fluid and so light, she makes it look like dancing this way, while also flying, is very easy. Her clips will go viral online in no time. Thumbs up. Thumbs down. Watching her, it feels as though you could be just like Carla, your foot stretched out and your back arched like a feline. And her smile, how easy would it be for you – for us – to smile like that and to seem happy like her? But then we can't.

The judges nod, Rachele is making a V for victory sign with her fingers, and every time Carla finishes an exercise she says 'Yes!' which is almost sweet. Carla is taking herself to the Olympics. She is *booking her ticket*. She is also making Rachele the best coach here.

I rub my head and smile before launching myself towards the bars. I am focused, lucid. I jump high and clean, but as soon as I get on, I feel a callous come off my hand at the second release move. The bar turns into a knife. My hand is now an open wound that hurts and is distracting me. I let go of the upper bar and in the fraction of a second that passes before grabbing the lower bar, I anticipate the pain I am about to feel. I imagine its intensity, like a whiplash across my face, invading my brain. I imagine it being so terrible that when I feel the actual pain, the one that comes from raw open skin, it is bearable. It's something I can do. So I do it. It's something I can bear, so I bear it.

Maybe it's my new short hair and maybe Dad has been right all along. We are happy, we love each other, and money doesn't matter one bit. Life is doable and it's OK to work nights, it's OK to cry and for our palms to weep, and this Sunday is my Sunday so I focus on my routine's magic, on the form, the technique and composition. I manage to enjoy it. Then, to love it. I embrace the pain and celebrate it. I land in what is a really good landing and I land as if I have just conquered Mars. I have. I raise my arms. I salute and I smile the biggest smile of all the known and unknown galaxies when I suddenly realize I'm smiling with my dad's mouth instead of my own and that I must look really ugly, and desperate.

So instead of enjoying the applause that follows, I rub my lips with my hand and erase it.

We wait for Nadia's score at the bars and for mine. I keep my fingers crossed, and hope my points will bring me up, and that the absence of Angelika will help us all in this too. Nadia gets a good 14.66. I receive another 14.4 and smile with my own smile, not my dad's one, and as nobody greets me, I go back to Rachele. I stand next to her and hope someone will remember I was here too, and that I too was good. That I am Martina with the biggest M in the world, I've been training for a thousand years, I've been falling and failing for a thousand years and I've been crying for a thousand years. I'm nailing it today, at my level, OK, but I am. *Tell me well done*, I think. *Just tell me.*

She doesn't.

Anna pats my shoulder. Maybe I said that I needed a pat out loud? Are we now all so out of control we don't even know if we are thinking or talking?

'You're doing so well,' Anna says. 'You've got this.'

'Thank you,' I say. 'How are you feeling?'

'My ankle hurts. And I won't make it in the first twenty.'

'You are getting better,' I lie.

'Promise?'

'Promise.'

I see Karl in the stands; he still has two hours to go before the boys compete and before we, the girls, are finished. He has come here to watch. Especially to watch her, Carla. Anna looks at him too but immediately lowers her eyes. She has always been this way; she lowers her eyes and maybe she thinks that this is how she is going to live longer.

I am fidgeting with my zip, rubbing my leotard as I try not to look at Karl. But then I do. His eyes won't leave Carla. And Nadia. Again Carla. Why is he here? After a little while Rachele notices his presence, the eyes of her girls moving towards him and his towards them, and she looks flustered. It's a question of superstition too. It's all going quite well and nothing is supposed to change. No new audience needs to come. No new problems need to come. No Karls are allowed. The hours have to go by quickly, Carla has to stay focused, the snow has to keep falling. Rachele has to stick to Alex's side and she has to keep standing because when things are going right and you are standing, then you must not sit down until the end of the competition. If things are going right and you are sitting down, then you don't get up until the end of the competition. But now Karl has come in, and things might change and maybe Karl will bring bad luck and maybe Carla will fall.

'Nadia is in love with Carla,' I say to Anna and Benedetta.

Anna lowers her eyes more. I wonder how low they can go, maybe to the very core of the Earth? In that moment I see her lowering her eyes and crying when she was 10, after getting her hands slapped by Vittorio. I see her getting driven home by her chauffeur, closing her eyes in the back seat, and crying after failing at the beam. Then crying with Carla, after she had pulled her hair so hard she screamed. I try hard to remember her laughing and manage to come up with the time we threw ourselves onto the mats singing cartoon theme tunes. There was another time at a regional championship, when we were 11 or 12, and her mother had come to watch. After, she had taken all of us out for a meal. That evening Anna was laughing and her mum must have thought her little girl was always happy.

'She really loves her a lot,' I say.

Why am I telling Anna and Benedetta? I really don't know, but the fact I have chosen to tell the Useless Ones must mean something. Maybe I'm just a coward. They won't say the wrong thing and they won't tell anyone. Or maybe we are friends?

'And Carla?' Benedetta asks. 'Does she love her back?'

'I don't know,' I say. And I truly don't know if she does.

Anna rubs her ankle. It is swollen and you can see at a glance that there is something wrong with it. I have never loved her as much. I manage to come up with another time she was laughing. It was while we were all dancing, after training, to the tunes of some new popstar's single.

'It's not that I don't want to tell you,' I say. 'I really have no idea.'

'I know,' Anna says. 'It's OK.'

Benedetta isn't a happy sight, shoulders slumping, sad face. She looks like she's making a show of being desperate, about to have a temper tantrum so she can get what she wants from her mum. She isn't competing today and she won't compete elsewhere much longer.

'The beam hates me,' she whines.

'Might do,' Anna says. Then lies, 'But the mat loves you.'

Benedetta is on the verge of tears, but she holds them shimmering inside her eyes. Every tear looks like a small fish in a tank. We have never been thrilled with her performance at the beam. Nor with her performance at the bars. It is now clear there are us four, then her. She is less skilful, less strong, less precise. With tantrums. She is also getting too thin.

'It's OK not to be a gymnast,' I say. And I am not sure if I am saying it to her or to me. 'Might actually be better.'

I drink two sips of water and stand up. I don't want my muscles to think it's over and go to sleep. I move towards the floor mat, where the Spanish doctor is trying to bend the leg of one of their athletes. The poor girl grits her teeth. It's making me feel sick so I look at the snow until they carry her away. Nobody pats her head or gives her a kiss. Three months' rest? One year? Out for good and all this pain was worth what?

'It's OK not to be a gymnast,' I could go and tell her too. Maybe in Spanish. *Esta bien*, then what?

Carla is celebrating her stunning 14.88 at the floor routine. The sum of her scores shows that she's leading the championship big time, and that she's about to become today's star. Even if the battle for gold is not yet over, they are shouting her name from the terraces. Nadia is mouthing, 'I love you' and some of the photographers' cameras are flashing. They light her up and when she realizes, she flexes her arm like Popeye. She really has found a good signature pose, with that arm thing. I smile, even though I see Nadia say 'I love you' again, and she is saying it to no one, because Carla is actually smiling at Karl in the audience. I shiver, then count to ten, to a hundred, and know we will be dogged by bad luck because Carla has not kept her promise to hate the letter K and to never again look at a K.

Where is Angelika with a K?

Nadia's expression doesn't change. I thought she'd get angry, that at the very least she would give them the finger, make a face, but maybe today is OK. Maybe bad luck is just silliness, maybe promises don't last long and the only thing that matters is what we are really able to do. Resist. Jump. Fly. Win.

The Romanian club is keeping up with the pace, without excelling spectacularly, but with a unique cleanliness, and no major errors. They no longer have Angelika but they are still very strong. They are probably thinking of their star all the time as they glance around, expecting her to walk in at any moment, but they're keeping it together. Maybe they are even praying for her, while also being good little soldiers. Good little girls. Their coach Tania is inscrutable, her back straight, a delicate smile on her lips. Her face is a blank sheet of paper on which you can read either good or evil, depending on how you feel. If you were in a good mood you could draw laughter on it.

Nadia comes to stroke my head. Carla copies her. Again.

'Do you remember that dog of a Romanian coach who kicked his gymnast in the belly?' Carla asks, caressing my head too. 'The pisser?'

I nod. First because Carla often adds the word 'pisser' to the word 'Romanian'. Just like the Polish girls always add *mafiosi* to any Italian name. Second, because when I heard about the gymnast that peed herself at the bars, I knew I'd never be able to forget it. When she'd finished her exercise, the coach had intercepted her on her way out and – thinking they were probably hidden enough in the arena's corridor – he had kicked her so hard, she doubled up in pain.

'They are mad,' Carla says. 'And that girl was a pisser. I bet they've tortured Angelika a bit too much and broken her.'

'Picture her with sticks in her mouth.' Nadia giggles, remembering Carla's abracadabra.

And her voice is the same as when she sees things.

Anna's music for her floor routine begins. I watch her acrobatic sequence. Then her backward somersault. She's doing well but I can see how her sore ankle is affecting her performance. I follow the shadow of her body and realize she too has got really thin. She must have not touched food this week. But then again, it may have happened in the last two hours. If we put our minds to it, we are able to lose weight in one day. You just have to stop drinking water.

Knowing she shouldn't give any more attention to Anna – she's a lost cause now – Rachele goes up to Nadia. I can smell Rachele's lipstick from here, her hairspray, her shampoo. Her lies.

'Nadia,' she says. 'What's that face? You look like you've seen a ghost.'

Carla is behind us. She's done with her spectacular competition and she now sits in silence, praying, her eyes fixed on the scoreboard. I am sure she's reminding God she's his angel and her enemies need to disappear from her path to glory.

My back aches, my feet and most of my hand are in pain too, and it's worse where the callous got ripped off. I want to pour disinfectant on it, feel a terrible sharp pain, then nothing. I try to pray some invented prayer then I quit. I lack the alphabet. The gods.

'Nadia, you are OK,' Rachele says. 'I wanted to let you know you are mathematically OK.'

'Why are you telling me that?' she says.

'I'm telling you so you won't be scared. You are OK, you are in the first ten.'

She really can't hack it any longer, our coach. Or maybe she has never been able to and we were just too young to notice. Her words sound wrong, in all sorts of ways. I add the numbers up again and in fact Nadia is not OK at all. Carla is at well over 60 already and *she* is OK. But Nadia still has to do her floor routine, where she needs at least 14.50 to be in the first ten.

Nadia must have done the sums too, because she twists her face towards her shoulder, like a dog when hearing an unfamiliar noise.

'You're lying,' she tells Rachele. 'You are a liar. Stop doing that!'

'You know Rachele's a liar deep down,' Carla sneers.

Rachele knows we could all attack her now. She knows what we are talking about. I can see her guilt. Her worry. Alex is pale too. The whole world is pale and the whole world is guilty. We could push both of them on the podium, defendants of their trial, and accuse them and judge them and destroy them in front of everyone. *There, get your medals*, we would say. And we would throw at them medals that would feel like stones.

'Carla,' Rachele says. 'Let's all calm down.'

Carla doesn't even look at her. She keeps her eyes only on Nadia.

'The only bit of truth, though, Nadia,' Carla says, 'is that if you make it to the first ten, you have to take your clothes off as promised. If you bring home a disgusting 13.50, a beggar's 14 or worse, you can leave the club without looking back. See if the Spanish take you with them.'

'You're a bitch,' Nadia says.

But she smiles. Rachele smiles too. I wish all her teeth would fall out.

'Doing it for you, my love.'

They hug so tightly, I look away, and so do Anna and Benedetta.

'You're right. Promises are promises, a pact is a pact,' Nadia says. 'A lie is a lie, and K is dead and K is not dead.'

'And dogs are dogs and the snow is supposedly still snow. Whatever. Now turn your sexy butt around and show us what you can do,' Carla says. 'Go crush them.'

Rachele must be feeling left out so she says again, 'Show us what you can do, Nadia.'

I stick my nails into my hands and grit my teeth so hard I feel them powder on my tongue. Nadia walks to the floor and her legs look stiffer than usual, moving like doll's legs. The light in here has never seemed as bright. As Nadia walks to the mat, she is showing us her arched little back exactly like I've seen her do a thousand or a million times. I see her past. Her present. If I keep on watching I will probably see her future too, her body in her leotard, putting on weight, growing big.

The music starts and as Nadia starts moving, I close my eyes. When I open them again she is vaulting. A *Tsukahara*. An *Arabian layout*. Carla clenches her fists and Rachele chews harder on her gum. In the stands Karl stands up to see better and I feel sorry for him. Maybe this afternoon I will help him understand.

'There's no place for you here,' I'll tell him. 'Run away from them and from us as fast as you can.'

I see a couple of policemen walk up to Karl. I look

again and I see another three near the jury and another one walking towards us.

'Look,' Anna says. 'Police, everywhere.'

Nadia finishes her impressive performance with a lean double full; only a small hesitation then her feet land strongly on the ground. She gives a beautiful wave, a tear falls from her eye, Carla claps her hands.

She was great. I smile too.

Carla goes towards Nadia and Nadia looks at Karl, Carla, the police, the spectators, and at the jury. She looks at the snow outside, so much snow now you can no longer see the sky, the air, the present. She looks at the lights above us, at the cuts on her hands, at Rachele. Alex. She looks back at Carla, her only love, while her 14.70 appears on the scoreboard, so stunning it looks enormous, and so magnificent it gets her to 56.88. I start clapping with the others, until I see Nadia wink at Carla.

Then, I see Nadia pull off one of the sleeves of her pink leotard.

Over the years I have thought of at least twenty different ways of leaving gymnastics. Some nights, before falling asleep, I even prepare the speech I'd give. I choose the tone of voice and the look I want them to remember me by as *my look*. They will say, 'And then, when she started talking, she had *that look*.' I could choose to go in a spectacular way, shouting that they are all blind, we are slaves, adults abuse us, we could die every day to nail a *Tsukahara*. Other times I picture myself calm and very wise. A monk. I explain that even if this was my dream, competitions have nothing to do with me, that I feel a million light years away from them all, and the world is not the size of a gym. It isn't rectangular and the ground is not covered with lino. I ask them how come you can almost never open the windows in gyms? They are sealed shut or too high up or too big for us, so we can't let in the fresh air.

'There's fresh air outside, you know?' I'll whisper.

I'll add that many years ago, I heard Vittorio talking to his replacement, Rachele, and what I'd heard had terrified me. It was a simple anecdote but one I had kept in my mind for years, as I expected it to come in useful at some point in my life.

'Now, when I train the little ones,' he said, 'I pray not to come across real talent. I never want to meet another champion in my life and have to be responsible for leading them to a terrible life.'

'Come on,' Rachele said. 'We love gymnastics.'

'I feel sorry for them. You should feel sorry too.'

To have people feel sorry for you is not that great, I guessed.

And so, I'll say everything and I'll say it well. This is why I compose my speeches in the right order, one perfectly placed passage after the other, one carefully chosen word after the other. A twist in the plot and a tear, a reflection, followed by a fit of anger.

'There's fresh air outside,' I'll repeat. 'There's ultraviolet light.'

At which point they will most likely laugh and blow raspberries at me. Loudly. Nice fat raspberries, one after the other. But I will keep talking, adding I had heard the coach Vittorio say we are *victims* and that we were so short because we never got any direct light, so we were not able to synthetize vitamin D to help us fix the calcium in our bones.

'All in all, it isn't a miracle to be so small. It's more like a scientific experiment,' I'll say. 'We are *sick*.'

I'll then execute seven joyous handsprings and two triple somersaults in a row and maybe someone will cry and will remember me from that day on, forever.

But the next morning I don't want to stop anymore. And deep down I know that competitions have a lot to do with me too. I like being in a gym without ultraviolet light better than anywhere else. To be fair, I even like being afraid. Closed windows are not really a problem, and fresh air and light gets in through the doors anyway. When I do a good floor exercise, or nail a dangerous jump, it all falls back into place, including the words I say to myself on the bus home, in order to love that Tuesday too, and the Wednesday that will follow.

'This is your world, Martina. This is your family,' I say to myself. 'You never really leave your family.'

Staring at Nadia grabbing her pink sequinned sleeve, Carla looks as if she's about to faint. Her face has the kind of colour it gets when your blood pressure drops to fifty, thirty, ten. Her lips are dark, her skin is grey. Nadia, on the other hand, has red cheeks, one of those wide smiles of hers. The smiles she smiles when the stats are on her side, or when Carla gives her a hug or a kiss or anything really. I move next to Anna and Benedetta, who have moved next to Rachele.

'It's a bet,' I explain. 'Something they promised each other.'

They look at me in terror. The fear inside Rachele's pupils is the shape of the wolf we've all been looking for. Nadia pulls off the first sleeve and lets it dangle under her armpit. Her feet are still; her eyes are fixed on Carla's. She pulls off the second sleeve and spins around on herself. The sleeves lift up in the air, like a multi-coloured toy windmill. The other gymnasts at the bars look at her. I see some of the boys turn slowly towards Nadia and stand on their chairs to get a better view. I see phones being opened up on the terraces, video cameras pointing towards her. I see camera flashes. I see her tears. Rachele's.

Carla takes another step closer to Nadia. Maybe she wants to show her the Popeye arm. Or she wants to kiss her, in front of everybody, and our team will make history and we will be remembered through the centuries and the millennia, amen. I know she wants to fix it, Carla.

'Stop it,' she says. 'Now.'

'I promised, Carla. I'm mathematically in the first ten, so I will get naked.'

'You'll ruin us all like this.'

'So why did you make me promise?'

'I just wanted you not to be scared! To think of something else. Something stupid.'

'I never was scared. You were.'

'What are you? Dumb?'

'If I don't take my clothes off, it'll bring us bad luck.'

Nadia slips her fingers under the leotard's Lycra, near her breasts. Both sleeves are now hanging like elephant trunks, coming out of her armpit. I would like to give a cashew to those elephant trunks.

'Let's pretend you're just adjusting your leotard, OK?' Carla says. 'I'll help you. It still won't seem quite real, but it might distract attention.'

'I want to get naked. A promise is a promise.'

Carla looks at Nadia with hatred. She grabs her arm and holds it tight, like my mum used to when I didn't want to follow her. I'd feel her fingers sink into my biceps and when she'd finally let go I'd have red marks on my skin. I don't think Mum knew how tight she grabbed me. But she did squeeze hard and it did always hurt.

Carla unrolls a sleeve and pulls it back onto Nadia's hand, her arm. Then she does the same with the other one. She crouches down as if to check the back of the leotard and does it with such confidence that I find myself staring at the leotard to see what's wrong with it. Nadia lets Carla finish. Her cheeks are no longer red and she doesn't look happy any more.

'You've ruined the magic, Carla,' she whispers.

Nadia walks near her, her head down, back to the bench. She puts her tracksuit back on. We all do the same. Alex and Rachele talk to some of the journalists. Then among themselves. They push Carla forward for some shots. For questions and handshakes. Carla smiles. We smile too.

At the end of the day, we are so stoked we've done so well in the competition that we try to forget the leotard episode together with all the other episodes and monsters that haunt us. I was perfect at the beam and got a luminous 14.60. I have even done better than Nadia on it, and this, today, makes me the team's second best at balancing on the beam, just after Carla. Maybe Rachele will really decide to put me forward for the national team selection. Shame about my landing at the bars, sure, OK, and shame about my left foot, which would just not stay still, but I have given my best and we have all given our best and that best was seen. My trimmed hair has helped; so has the forest and the snow. Carla is today's gold medallist, Nadia is in the top ten, and I made it to number twelve, which for me is great. It's more than great, it's a revolution. Maybe Benedetta will not be with the rest of us at the Olympics, and Anna needs to work more on her self-esteem, but hey, who doesn't? We are in a state of grace, we are all alive, Nadia hasn't stripped in front of everyone, and for now we cannot wish for more.

'One body, one heart,' we all whisper.

When Carla walks to the podium, to receive her gold medal, we are all receiving it with her. The crowd is cheering, and goes wild as she does her Popeye move. Despite Nadia's sad eyes, we scream out our happiness. We all hug, then we go to the stands to sign autographs for the young girls who want to be us. We pass around Carla's medal and we kiss it one by one. We also kiss the club's flag, then we hug Rachele. Alex hugs us too but I leave my arms down, like Nadia's empty leotard sleeves.

Lying back on the arena's benches, we glare at the Chinese and Russian girls like sworn enemies, but we are already imagining them far away again, faraway thoughts of a faraway future. They existed here, during this week, and they had a space in our minds and in our hearts for this week. They can now disappear again.

'Ladies and gentlemen, we regret to inform you that the Romanian gymnast Angelika Ladeci has gone missing,' the announcer says over the loudspeakers. Then repeats it in Romanian. 'Please report any sightings of her and be vigilant. I repeat, gymnast Angelika Ladeci – blonde, one metre forty-five – is missing.'

The Romanian team is sitting in front of us. Their coach holds her chin high; she still has the most neutral look I've ever seen in my life. Is she desperate? Is she OK? Is she even a person and not a machine? Each one of their athletes is strong and as a team they definitely proved themselves to be stronger than us, than most other teams. But it's true, without Angelika they don't have a star and we do have a Carla.

'Good girls!' Rachele says. And hugs us more. 'Not to worry, and let's get changed now, OK?'

I swallow twice, shift my foot twice, and drum my

fingers on my knees, but the number two is starting to get on my nerves. It looks like a number one, if I think about it properly. A mirror image, revealing itself to be too balanced. I try to bite my lip three times and run my hands through my hair three times. I resist for a few seconds, embracing the change, embracing the revolution, but I have to balance the accounts immediately, starting over with multiples of two and with the repetitions of two. After ten repetitions, I still feel that deep down the harmony has been disrupted by the series of threes.

More police arrive. The judges are shaking their heads and furrowing their brows. When an announcement is made over the loudspeakers that the boys' competition is postponed, Rachele tells us it's time to go back to the hotel and that they will let us know about Angelika and the boys' competition as soon as there is any news.

We get into our puffer jackets. We slip into our boots.

'Does anyone fancy calling home?' She adds, 'And having a starter, main course, dessert, and maybe even double dessert for dinner? We need to celebrate.'

Nadia and Carla look at each other, smile. Maybe they do fancy dessert. And they for sure want to celebrate.

'Love Romania,' Carla says. 'Will love it forever and ever. Amen.'

'Amen,' we all repeat.

'All fancy a hot shower now?' Rachele says.

I think of hot jets of water over my head, massaging my shoulders. I definitely fancy that. I'll turn the pressure up and stand under it for at least ten minutes, knowing that this day is nearly over, that the competition didn't kill me or destroy me. And that we are bringing home some gold and the whole of our team in one piece. Monday I'll be back to my fears, but today I can rest.

'I fancy the shower,' I say.

I cover my head with the hood and follow the team.

We step into the freezing cold and the snow under our feet is so soft that I feel like we are still on the mat, ready to jump. I smile, but the wind blows so hard I have to wipe away tears from the cold.

'Walk in a line behind me and don't disappear,' Rachele says. 'It's getting dark and we're worried enough about Angelika.'

'We're worried too,' says Carla, without sounding worried.

'In the meantime, keep your eyes peeled on our way to the hotel, OK?' Alex says.

'Let's keep our eyes peeled!' Carla bursts out. 'We're definitely going to be of help keeping our eyes peeled.'

She starts pretending to be something with sharp eyes and a fast-swivelling neck. A radar perhaps. Or a lynx. Rachele's teeth are chattering and I realize mine are too.

'I fancy a hot shower,' I say again.

'We know, hon,' Rachele says. 'You've said that already.'

It is still snowing hard and the teams and the police disappear in all that white. It has never been so cold and the snow is almost up to our knees. The two man-bears with the coats must be overworked by now, maybe not even laughing any more. I think that they might be my favourite people in the whole world.

Although I'm freezing, every breath reminds me that we have done well in the competition. And that the tournament is finished so I can stop visualizing the thousand different ways it could go. Tonight I will sleep deep and, once awake again, I will be able to think of other things. At dinner I will eat as much as I want, carbs, cheese, two desserts maybe, yes, definitely two, and tomorrow we'll go home and I almost look forward to it. I can finish a half-done puzzle with Dad. I can be their good mouse in the mousy house at least for a day or two.

'Let's hurry,' says Anna. 'It's freezing.'

Benedetta and Rachele pick up the pace. Carla follows, Alex by her side.

'You were amazing out there,' he tells her. 'You were the best by far.'

'Thank you. It felt great.'

'We are a great team,' he adds. 'One body, one heart.'

'I guess,' Carla says. And looks the other way.

I have to decide if I should walk slowly like Nadia or fast like all the others. But the other group has Alex in it, so I'm better off alone. I look at the sky and snow crystals fall into my eyes. There's about five minutes to go until dark.

'Martinaaa,' Carla shouts. 'Martinaaa,' she shouts again.

'Martinaaa,' and it is still Carla.

'What?' I yell, and run towards them.

One of the Romanian athletes is behind us, and falls in the snow. Tania the coach shouts at her, so we look. The girl is crying. The coach is very near her and pushes her to get up. See, Tania is not so unreadable. And she is officially not so sweet.

Carla comes to my side.

'Maybe she hits Angelika,' she says. 'She's so violent.'

'I guess,' I say. Mimicking her voice of just a few seconds ago.

Some teams remind me of those films with soldiers shouting in each other's faces. But maybe the Romanians are also acting, to look stronger and tougher, and this might be a scene they are putting on, just for us. Later, in secret, they will all laugh and hug each other.

'Do you think she ran away?' I ask Carla. 'Maybe her

physiotherapist touches her too. And that's why that gymnast is now crying.'

'You nutter. Maybe her teammate is crying because right now she hates Angelika,' Carla continues. 'She let them all down today.'

We are near the bridge and the police are switching on their torches to search the field ahead. A few beams reach all the way to where we are; other rays of light are like glow-worms lying on the buildings and the dark forest.

'God has helped us,' Cara says, 'Amen.'

'Amen,' we all repeat. And I am not sure if this guilt-soaked 'amen' will stick with us forever.

Nadia trots towards us. She is smiling and when I smile back, she winks at me. I copy her with my left eye only. But because of having to do things in sequences of twos, I have to wink again with the right one. I get mixed up, botch it, and feel sort of sad for myself.

'Now we slow down,' Carla whispers in my ear.

'We? Who?'

'Me, you, and Nadia.'

'But why?'

'Because we'll slow down, jog towards the darkness, then stop and hide for a few minutes. As soon as the coast is clear, we'll go and look for Angelika.'

My heart jumps. Like when I'm between a bar and the next, between galaxies, like when I'm with Carla and Nadia.

'Not only gold medallists and top-ten gymnasts, but heroes too. Wouldn't that be great?' Carla says.

'I guess,' I repeat.

'Stop doing that "I guess" thing.'

Ahead of us, Rachele is talking a mile a minute to Alex and they keep on saying 'Yes! Yes! Yes!' Anna laughs and when Alex shouts 'Yes!', I slow down. I slow more, as

Rachele recites again the list of the medals we got. They are walking fast because of the cold, and they are soon far ahead. Rachele turns round just once, and all three of us give her the thumbs up. She replies with the same gesture and seems content with that. I can still change my mind. If I don't want to follow Carla and Nadia, I just have to run towards Anna and I'd catch up with Rachele and Alex in a blink.

'Do you want to let her freeze to death?' Carla asks me when she sees me hesitate.

I shake my head. I want to be a hero and I don't want Angelika to freeze to death. I also don't want to join Alex or hear him say 'yes'. The police are here, the shovelling bears are here; how could we possibly be the ones that find her? And aren't Carla and Nadia afraid of wolves?

'So do you want her death to be your fault?' Carla adds.

'No. But I'm freezing.'

'Don't talk crap. I'll take care of you and will warm you up whenever you want.'

Carla, Nadia, and I slow down. Everyone disappears in seconds.

'Ten, nine, eight, seven, six, five,' Carla counts.

At four, we can still hear their voices. At two, the voices are gone. At one, Carla grabs our hands, and we run towards the nothingness. The snow muffles all sounds. The wind erases them forever. When we get a few dozen metres away, we crouch down in the dark. Carla and Nadia are still holding hands and I'm silently cursing my feet for going the wrong way, for not running towards Rachele, towards my warm shower and the double dessert. I need to pee, and in this posture, I am reminded of it every second.

'Beautiful night,' Carla says after a while. 'So romantic.'

'Lots of stars,' says Nadia. 'I also ordered this mega moon to celebrate your gold medal and our glorious finals.'

Carla and Nadia get up. We start walking back towards the gym and we border the forest. We bend down to make ourselves even smaller and even more invisible to the police torches that might catch us. We go down the valley, pretending to be snakes and ghosts, then we straighten up when we get to the bridge again. We walk more, slowly at first, then faster, and the rhythm of our steps on the metal is the same as that of our heartbeats.

While they have their backs to me, I try to send a text to Mum and Dad, without looking at the phone. I write that the competition has gone well. A hug, I write to Dad. Mouse of all Mouses. A kiss to Queen Mouse, I type. I put the phone back in my pocket and catch up with the girls.

'Snail,' says Carla. 'Tiny, lazy snail.'

My steps become their steps again, until Nadia stops halfway across the bridge. I think she might want to mock me or take the piss because she has seen me send the texts, and I am not obeying them or being fast enough. But then I realize she isn't even looking at me.

'It's freezing, stupid,' Carla says to her. 'Move.'

Nadia doesn't answer and doesn't move. I've had quite enough of her manias, her standby modes, and of this stupid idea of looking for Angelika. It is getting dark and we've been competing all day. Carla has given Karl up, we are back to being winners, and Nadia is still punishing her. Enough already.

'Nadia, your period will stop in this cold,' Carla says. 'The blood will freeze in your belly. Off we go.'

Nadia breathes in, then she runs towards the edge of the bridge. She runs as if she's going to vault over it, into the oncoming cars. My mouth falls open.

'Nadia!' I hear myself shout. 'Nadia!'

I look around, to see what she thinks will act as her uneven bar or her vault. She could grab anything and launch herself up to the starless sky. Carla and I won't be able to see her in the dark, but maybe a torch will light her up and then her fall will be spectacular. She'll probably choose to take her leave with a straight *Thomas*. She'll go up. Down. And we will hear a smash on the highway. Then, just silence.

I don't want to watch her die. I absolutely do not want to watch her die.

'Nadia!' Carla shouts.

I let out another scream and turn away. I count to two, maybe I don't even get to two, and from under us a lorry blows its horn and other cars hoot. I wait for the screeching of brakes. For the sound of her smashed body on the concrete down there. But the sound doesn't arrive. I hear another honk. If Nadia has jumped she will have caused an accident. The horns stop honking and I hear Carla take a run-up too. I turn round, with my eyes still closed. The Sunday of Revolution and Wonder is ending in a terrible way.

Then, ready to faint, to vomit, to scream, I open my eyes and Nadia is still there. She has stopped, on the verge of the bridge, her chest squeezed on the railing, the sky now black before her, and the vibrating echo of the horns now silent all around us. Maybe it was Carla snapping her fingers to break the spell, or pronouncing some kind of formula to undo the abracadabra. Maybe Nadia stopped before that and she never wanted to die.

'Dickhead,' Carla says.

Nadia turns round and smiles. She is panting. Her chest

is going up and down, lifting up her coat. Her breath is making a million tiny clouds in the air.

'What did you think I was going to do?' she asks.

'You scared me, fuck off.'

'You thought I was going to kill myself.'

'You wish, psycho.'

We start walking again. Carla's chin is trembling, but she pretends nothing has happened. That's what we always do, so we do it now too. We go down some steps at the side of the bridge and get near the forest. Our feet are in the snow, and the snow is up to our knees. Then our hips. I touch the tip of my nose and find a snowman's nose. It is a carrot now, so I touch it a second time to make it become my nose again.

'Stop that!' Carla says. 'You girls are fucking crazy. What's worse is that you don't even realize it.'

'My nose was a carrot for a second,' I say.

'Of course it was. Happens to me all the time.'

And she laughs, as we hear police sirens coming closer. We stay in the dark and we watch as some of the other teams and their coaches walk in line towards the hotel, their rooms, the heat, the hot showers, and the possibility of double desserts. I catch sight of the bears in their coats, who like us are looking around, and calling out Angelika's name. The policemen are saying to each other, 'We'll go this way. You go that way.' Karl, handsome but like a stiff plastic toy, goes past the police and towards the hotel. Nadia points deeper into the forest.

'That way?' I ask. 'Are you sure?'

'Yes, I am sure, Carrot Nose.'

Carla nods and we take a run-up, watching out for the teams, the police, everyone. We avoid their torch blazes and, faster than the light, faster than their steps and voices, we launch ourselves towards the trees. We get the giggles. But then we look around and can't see a thing. We switch on our phone torches.

'Where are we?' I ask.

'*Where are we?*' they whine, mocking me.

Carla grabs Nadia's hand and starts walking quickly into the woods, following the beam of her torch. Every bit of her reminds us that even out here, she is the boss. And even out here, she is our gold medallist. Not to give her any more satisfaction, I stop talking and promise myself I will never ask her for anything at all, ever, for as long as I live.

We reach the thickest part of the woodland and we hear voices shouting 'Angelika!' and others shushing them loudly, hoping to be able to hear her voice, her pleas for help. We walk along a beaten track where the trees are getting taller.

'I want to go back to the hotel,' I say, forgetting my promise to never talk again.

Carla points the torch at my eyes. My pupils contract so fast I feel them stinging.

'I want to go back to the hotel,' she says, copying me again, making my words sound stupid.

She keeps on walking, so I do too. To make it even clearer that she's mocking me, she takes her hat off and puts it back on twice and zips her jacket down and up twice. She says, 'Who am I, hey?' Nadia and I don't say anything so, after a few more tries, Carla stops having a go at me and starts playing with the torch's light. Nadia seems tired, more tired than me.

'Do you feel like you're going to faint?' I ask.

She doesn't answer. The week is almost over and Carla and Nadia want to fix things and first of all they need to get away from boring little Martina and go back to being just the two of them against everyone else. But why did Carla insist on taking me into the woods with them if they hate me so much? We'll all get punished for sure. Unless we really do find Angelika. Then we'll be forgiven and will be famous throughout the universe and make history. Us, the good girls. In the pictures Carla will do the Popeye arm. Nadia will bow. I will do the head stroking with the humble smile.

'It was the right thing to do,' we'll declare.

The forest gets darker and thicker and Carla stumbles on a tree root. We see her vanish behind a heap of snow as she lets out a scream. Nadia squeezes my hands. We walk towards Carla, but without her torch to help us, it's hard. I can feel Nadia's breath in my ears and I want to ask her again if she is about to faint. Her breathing is strange, like a dog's. I imagine her with a really long tongue, like a Doberman's. I'd give her water. Meat. We get to the tree root and step over it and as we lean down to look for her, Carla jumps on us from behind a little hill of snow.

'Woah!' Carla yells, and jumps up and down with her arms spread out and the torch pointing up under her chin. 'Woah!' she yells again.

'Fuck off!' I scream. 'You bastard!'

Nadia is furious. She pushes Carla and takes the phone from her. She storms off and starts walking away from us and we follow, Carla still giggling. I am getting over the shock so I feel like laughing too as the rush of fear has woken me up completely. After all, it isn't so bad to be strolling in the woods, or to be making jokes that scare us for a second or two, and this too is a good adventure, a good backdrop, one of many I will have in the future, all over the world. In forests, in hidden warm clean lakes where I will bathe naked, and in never-ending lands where I will live on my own. I need to learn how to build a house, and light a fire.

Nadia is walking faster and faster, and to keep up with her we almost have to run. The branches are low, snow weighing them down like they are sad. When we reach a clearing, Carla lifts her arms and from where I stand it looks like she is holding the mega moon Nadia has ordered for her in her hands, and she could touch it if she jumped high enough. Today she has won everything and today we can all believe anything.

'Let's go back to the hotel!' says Carla suddenly. 'We've been nice enough to Angelika the dog. Besides, I'm hungry and thirsty. And none of this is fun.'

Nadia has stopped by a tree. Carla goes to hug her and Nadia doesn't move.

'We really must make you better, crazy little one,' she tells her. 'You're in bits. And I'm bored.'

I picture Nadia in bits right there on the snow. A tooth. A finger. Bits of her eye and her head. A foot and all the single hairs from her eyelids laid out in a row against the white. Then, Carla lets out a scream and I hate that scream and can no longer stand it, her, or the jokes.

'I've had it,' I say. 'I'm off.'

I want to get under the duvet and listen to music. I want easy things, normal and warm. We are gymnasts, OK, our life is kind of hard and messed up, OK, but now we are really going too far. Here is where I draw the line. But then I see Carla put her hand over her mouth so I turn to look in the same direction. Nadia is crying and I can see Carla is shaking, so I screw up my eyes and look closer, until I see Angelika tied to a tree. Her face is hanging down and her hair is over her forehead. Beside her is one of the shovels of the bears with coats. She isn't moving. Her legs are buried in snow, her arms bound by ropes. Bandages actually, the kind we put on our hands and feet during training. The same ones the Chinese kid used to commit suicide in her shower.

Angelika, I think. *We've found you.* Her bound arms are actually just one arm.

My legs have turned to stone. And ice. I no longer know how to move them. But Nadia and Carla remain still so I grab one of my legs, then the other, and walk towards Angelika. I cannot stand her being there, alone, still and so cold. Most of all, the snow over her legs seems an unbearable torture. Are the legs two?

'Angelika?' I say. 'Are you OK?'

Carla follows me, her hand still over her mouth. Nadia is crying behind us and I want to stop her, for real, forever. Amen.

'Be quiet, Nadia!' I say. 'Shut up.'

I kneel and see that the snow has been falling on Angelika for so long that it's now up to her belly. I lift her head and look away immediately. I throw up. Carla and I shovel the snow with our hands, like dogs digging for a bone, then with the bear's shovel, and we pull her leg out.

'What's wrong with her?' Carla asks me, crying.

She can only look down. I'm the only one now looking at Angelika's destroyed face. Under my fingers I can also feel a crack in the skull. I throw up again and put my hands back on her. I lift up her face and Carla now looks too. The face is white. Blue. And broken.

'What the fuck is wrong with her?' she screams. 'Is she dead?'

I think of the wolves in the forest and of the words

tear her to pieces. I think of them with Anna's voice. Carla is retching but nothing comes up.

'Oh my God,' she repeats. 'Who did this?'

She sticks her fingers in the elastic bands, rips them with her teeth, and manages to untie Angelika and tries to hold her upright. Her face is scratched, there's blood on her cheeks. Part of one eye is bluer than the rest of her face. Some bits are missing. Under the snow, her hair is matted with blood, her nose covered in bruises and scabs.

'A wolf starts from the belly,' Anna had explained to us. 'That is what they like.'

I will absolutely not look at her belly. I don't want to touch it and I don't want to know. I look at my hands and Angelika's blood has not stained them. Maybe this is a dream. Maybe it's one of our rhymes and abracadabras, pure imagination.

'Her blood hasn't stained me, maybe we're in a dream,' I say out loud, and immediately regret letting out such idiotic words. I look more closely and half my jacket is covered in blood. My hands too are now stained. Everything seems darker; the moon has disappeared. So have our souls.

'Go and get the police!' I shout to Nadia. 'Go and get someone!'

But she doesn't move. And she doesn't look at me. She looks at Carla instead.

'Red red yellow blue – Coca-Cola Fanta glue – teeth straight feet straight – me me but it's you – blue pooh Fanta glue – I protect and so do you,' she says.

'For fuck's sake, Nadia,' Carla shouts. 'Not now! Go fucking get someone!'

'Red red yellow blue – Coca-Cola Fanta glue – teeth

192

straight feet straight – me me but it's you – blue pooh
Fanta glue – I protect and so do you,' Nadia repeats.

Carla stands up, her legs shaking. She gets near Nadia.
I cannot move. I cannot breathe and I don't want to be
left alone in the forest with Angelika. Are these slashes
from a wolf's paws and claws? Will the wolves come and
eat my legs too? I try to look at her again. I see her
mouth is full of sticks; near her are the scissors we used
to cut my hair. I close my eyes again. *Picture her with
sticks in her mouth*, I remember Carla saying to Nadia.
I look at Nadia.

'You asked me to,' she is saying.

'What? What did I ask you?' Carla says. 'Shut up!'

'To put sticks in her mouth and spit in her eyes until
she's blind.'

Carla takes a step back and looks at me, at Angelika.
Then at Nadia again.

'Aren't you going to say anything, Popeye? I had to be
as strong as you to win her over. Had to smash her head
with that shovel first.'

Nadia copies Carla's Popeye move. Carla moves another
step back, Nadia moves a step closer and pushes her.
Then she says sorry.

'About what?' Carla says, slowly. 'What are you sorry
for?'

'Pushing you? Just now?'

Carla starts crying harder. She is shaking her head now
and huddling tighter inside her jacket. She is very cold
now and I have never seen her as hunched.

'Keep your back straight!' our coach would tell her.
'You look like an old lady! Keep your belly in. Don't be
such a drama queen.'

But there are no coaches here. It's only us.

'What have you done?' Carla mutters. Then she screams it again. 'What have you done?'

'I love you, Popeye.'

Carla screams more, as if something has cut her. She falls to her knees, sobbing so hard I can't bring myself to sob too. It's like she's doing it for everyone. Nadia pats her on the back. On the head. She looks proud, like when my cat offered me a dead lizard. The prey was for me. It was a present.

'I hit her head when she was running. I stabbed her with the scissors,' Nadia explains. 'I tied her up. The sticks in the mouth came after.'

'You make me sick! You are sick!' Carla says.

'I did it for you. For us and for the team. The wolves must have helped me too. Cute.'

I hold Angelika tight because it seems to be the only safe thing to do, the only place to be. I stay here even when Carla runs away and Nadia stands in front of me, watching Carla run away.

'Are you OK?' she asks me in her sweetest voice.

I nod and when she leaves, I hunker down deeper, and I pee. I wet myself and for a moment it feels warm, comforting, and the right thing to be doing. I am suddenly so tired I could lie down here and sleep, on Angelika's destroyed lap. I search my pockets. I want to call Mum, but can no longer feel my hands. It's probably the cold. Or the end of my life. My pee is now stinging under my trousers, behind my knees. I imagine Angelika dying and have to immediately stop. I imagine Nadia in prison. In front of the police.

'One day I will tell the police about Alex,' Nadia had told me and Carla a couple of years ago.

She had been the only one to come with me to Rachele

and that had clearly not worked. She had gone back to her alone, a few times, and that hadn't worked either. Carla had rolled her eyes even back then.

'Good girl, try that,' Carla had said. 'Let's see what silence will follow even then.'

'Would you really do it?' I had asked Nadia. 'Would you be brave enough to tell the police?'

'If I find myself with a gentle policeman, yes. Of course.'

I immediately thought that she would never find herself with a gentle policeman. Still, it felt better than nothing. It felt like something we could hope for. Hang on to.

'Thank you,' I had said.

'Why would you ever thank me?' She had laughed.

I scratch myself and Angelika's head slips and comes to rest against me. I straighten it and get up. If I leave, I am bad, but if I stay I will freeze. My feet are starting to ache, my face too. I slap my cheeks twice and it feels like I don't have cheeks. I have a hole there, like Angelika maybe has in her belly. I try to lift her up again, to hoist her over my shoulders. She is light, really light, but she is stiff and I cannot hold onto her. My feet sink in the snow under her weight and mine. I can't see anything, so I lay her down and cover her with my puffer jacket.

'I'll go and get someone,' I tell her, even if she can't hear me. 'I'll be back.'

I start running. It's snowing harder and I've had enough of this snow and of this running and falling. Of all these words, this pain, and all of this fear. I've had enough of this Sunday, of us. I clench my fists and don't feel a thing. Not only has my face gone numb, but so have my hands, and my heart. I feel myself running with my father's face in place of mine. When I was little my father used to still go and train. His saggy cheeks wobbled and he kept his mouth open. Every step rebounding all the way to his lips, every acceleration making him breathe faster.

'The cheapest sport in the whole world,' he used to say. 'You don't even need shoes.'

I'd watch him from the window, he'd smile at me. I had pictured him dying with that same smile on a thousand times. I had pictured him killing himself and leaving a suicide note with the words 'I'm happy' on it. Sometimes his note would have his handwriting, sometimes mine.

Tomorrow I will tell him it is over. My lies, his lies. I know he isn't happy. He knows I am not happy. I know he is scared and he knows I am scared. I feel his breath right in my ears and I chase it away with my hand.

As I run in the snow, feeling my feet about to give in, the hotel lights get closer and after my father's face falls from mine, I can still hear his steps behind me alongside Alex's, Angelika's, and Nadia's. Of all the coaches I've had to this day. Vittorio. Rachele. Their hands, their voices. Alex's hands, Alex's voice. All of the adults' voices of the world.

I come out from the woods to the front of the hotel and Carla is holding onto Karl. When she sees me, she moves away and runs over to Rachele. They are all out here, all probably still looking for Angelika. Carla is sobbing. Her back, shoulders, and head are shaking.

Nadia, still far in the distance, is walking in the snow towards them. Carla tries to look at her but can't and hides her face again between Rachele's breasts, in the shadow of that mega fringe of hers, now frozen with cold and terror. I know exactly what the smell is like so close to the coach and to her tits. The few times Rachele has held me I felt the same texture, the exact same smell of sweat, lotion, deodorant. Will Carla tell her? Or is the team, the competition, the Olympics, more important? Is Nadia's murder our murder?

One body, one heart.

The police are not following Nadia and nobody is going after her. Maybe Carla hasn't found the words yet. She holds on tight to her gold medal and cries harder. Alex hugs her. She pushes him away. I see a flash, then another one. Carla is now crying facing the cameras of the few journalists still here from the competition, resting only one side of her head on Rachele. Her mascara is running, making her black cheeks shine.

The shovelling bears with coats are standing perfectly still and like me they are now looking at Nadia, while the teams, in their coloured uniforms, assemble in the yard, the gel in their hair glinting in the dark. The police sirens fall silent, but the lights on the car roofs are flashing and change the colour of the snow, of the sky, of the faces of those who are closest to the road.

Of my face. Of Nadia's.

We go red. Then blue.

A memory of fireworks one stifling August fills my head. With Mum and Dad. We had climbed onto some old containers, Mum laughing as we pointed our chins to the sky to watch the colours explode. A terrible heat came up through my feet. I thought my shoes would melt. Mum kept saying, 'How nice it is here!' Dad held one of her hands in his, and mine with the other. At dawn, as we walked home, I lingered behind, watching as Mum stumbled, her heels cracked and bleeding.

'Best night of my life,' she had said. And as she said it again, her heels started bleeding more.

I feel sick and fall backwards into the snow. Nadia moves

a few more steps and takes her coat off. She stops and pulls off her shoes, her trousers. Carla turns around and the camera flashes turn with her and the teams have eyes only for Nadia now. She is taking off her jumper, her T-shirt. Rachele puts her hands over her mouth. I hate her. Why didn't she listen? Why didn't she stop our bodies and our minds from breaking? This is all their fault. I imagine Nadia's mother saying, 'My mistake has made a mistake.'

The flashes of light from the cars and the torches draw their blue and red lines on Nadia's skin. On and off again, like a lighthouse beam. Rachele is about to go to Nadia but Carla whispers something to her and our coach opens up her eyes wide. Carla has said it. What words did she use? Murder? Assassin?

The police lights make Rachele's face look even more monstrous.

I think of Angelika with bruises on her face, without a belly. And no one to protect her. Yesterday. Or ever. I think of her covered with my jacket and know she would not be happy to end her life under a rival team's flag. I have to tell someone where she is. I have to get her somewhere warm. And out of that flag.

I have to tell someone where we all are and get us all out of this flag.

Nadia takes a few more steps, five, maybe six. Then she stops, perfectly still and straight, her bottom sticking out like only ours do, her spine gleaming in the light. She looks like a child.

'I need to speak with a gentle policeman,' she says.

I hope the mega moon will fall on her head, our head, make her vanish – make us vanish – now, forever. Amen.

'Fall, moon,' I say out loud. 'Fall!'

But nothing happens.

Nadia pulls down one of the pink sleeves of her leotard, then the other, and rolls it all off. From behind, we see her naked and so tiny, on the snow that doesn't even seem cold any more. She kneels and becomes even smaller, a head and a few centimetres of the smallest back in the world, of the smallest body in the world, while everything goes quiet. There is silence, everywhere. We all stop breathing at once and seen from above we must look like we are posing for a photograph, so many of us and no movements, not a single foot shifting. Not a single breath.

Just click. Flash. Click.

My phone vibrates. Then it starts ringing with the usual ring tone, the one that makes me feel ashamed. I grab it and see it is Dad. I let it ring in my hand, and the name *Dad* keeps flashing on and off again. I don't know what to do with the phone and with the word Dad. When it finally stops, I put it back in my pocket. I look at Nadia, now completely naked in the snow, her pink leotard near her. I look at Carla crying and Rachele with that hand over her mouth.

I am cold. And I am very, very tired.

I turn around and go towards the hotel. I walk to the entrance, go past the bears with the coats who are not laughing anymore. They aren't moving either. It is possible everyone is on pause and I am the only one able to switch to play. If I shout, no one will turn around. If I cry, no one will comfort me.

'She hit her with your shovel. She tied her up. She put sticks in her mouth. And maybe a wolf ate her belly,' I tell the bears. 'But she'd been hurt too. And wolves ate our bellies too. Since forever.'

The bears don't look at me. Maybe I haven't even spoken out loud; my mouth has not opened and it probably is not even there anymore. I don't have the strength to check, so I don't run my hand over my lips or try to fix it. If I no longer have a mouth, there is nothing I can do about it and there is nothing I can fix.

In the foyer, I turn back one last time and watch as the police move towards Nadia. I really hope she finds the gentle one. I call the lift but don't wait for it. I take the service stairs and walk up to our room and look at Nadia's bed, her bag, the leotards. I sit on the mattress and switch on the bedside lamp. In the mirror I see a head of closely cropped hair and the face of someone who looks an awful lot like me but who surely isn't me. I switch the lamp off.

'People are disgusting,' Carla had said to Nadia last night.

It was just a few hours before, now I knew, Nadia had left the room, the war-hotel, and had chased Angelika in the woods during her run.

'They always have flaws. Spots. BO. Or they look pathetic from behind. If you stare up close, at their pores for example, or at their cracked enamel, everyone fails. That way nobody scares you anymore.'

'If someone is good but fails, they don't threaten you?'

'They only make me sick.'

'Angelika doesn't have spots,' Nadia had said. 'And she doesn't seem to fail.'

'Angelika is yellow. And she is a freak. Totally disgusting. Also, I hope she dies.'

We had laughed. Even though Angelika wasn't yellow at all. Even if we often felt like freaks and had spots too. And even if, as usual, we had brought in death. Carla had laid on top of Nadia and Nadia had said she liked it, because it must be pleasant to have someone's weight on you, legs on legs, skin against skin. It must be beautiful to let your back be loosened by someone you love. Thanks to their pleasure, I had felt the same pleasure and some of their love.

'Tell me your five favourite things in the universe,' Nadia had asked her.

'Gymnastics. You. The sea. Winning. I can't think of a fifth. Tell me yours.'

'Gymnastics. You. Mum.'

'Mum?' Carla had exclaimed. 'Did you really say Mum?'

Carla had repeated another million times, 'Mum? *Mum*?', pressing down on her more and more. Nadia, trapped under Carla, was laughing so hard she could hardly breathe. I laughed with them, trying to make myself heard, before closing my eyes and thinking of my five favourite things in the universe.

My first one too was still gymnastics.

Acknowledgements

No book is ever the work of one person alone. This one in particular is the result of many voices gathered over many years. It is also the result of many ideas of different people, who have looked at gymnastics and at our girls' week and lives – at this story – in a way that was often radically different from mine. *Corpo Libero* or *The Girls Are Good* was published for the first time in 2010: it began life as a film for the director Martina Amati. We never made that movie, but the story belongs to her as well, as does the vision: thank you. This story also belongs to a coach whom I worked with for a long time and who – despite his immense love for this sport and coaching – was no longer able to accept the terrible things he witnessed. He entrusted me with his secrets and with his thoughts. He handed me his pain and that of the girls to care for, always and forever, while also giving me advice and his permission to expose some of the horrors he had seen. This book is also by all the gymnasts I have known and all those I have never met, but have observed and loved, from near and far, who have fallen and got up or, sometimes, did not get up again. The ones who enchanted me. Moved me. And broke me. Their voices – what I heard of those voices – are hopefully in these pages, and they have shaped and nurtured Martina's and the other girls' voices. Thank you. This story has now taken on a whole new dimension and meaning for me, thanks to all the gymnasts, whose names we now know, whose faces we now know, who – many years after the first publication of this novel, when all the horror was still being silenced – spoke loudly and forcefully, breaking through a wall that seemed indestructible. They have forged an immense revolution and we will always be grateful to them. Thank you, you are heroes.

This novel also exists thanks to those who have read, reread, written, and rewritten it with me hundreds of times for years: I am forever grateful to you.

To my editors: Alberto Rollo, who has been there since the beginning, to Linda Fava and to Gillian Stern who I hope will be there forever and are always my first and last readers. You are my allies and my teachers: thank you. To my Italian publishing house Mondadori who believed that going back to this story – years later – was right, and indeed, necessary. Thanks to Phoebe Morgan, my brilliant HarperCollins editor, who filled this new phase with energy, power, and magic: I'm very lucky you wanted this book. Elizabeth Sheinkman, my agent at Peter Fraser + Dunlop, who supports me, advises me, and laughs with me: thank you. Carmen Prestia, my agent at Alferj Prestia, who listens to my every idea and for every one of them has a better one: thank you. Ellie Game, who designed the stunning cover: thank you, I love it.

This story also exists thanks to the writers who are giving it new life in the TV adaptation: my forever sparring and shining partner Ludovica Rampoldi, the luminous and supernatural Chiara Barzini, and the very talented gymnast and writer Giordana Mari: you all improve the voice of everything, always, and fill the new life of the girls with light, wonder, and strength. I am in awe. Thanks to the unrelenting force and will of the producers: Nicola Giuliano, Carlotta Calori, Francesca Cima, and Viola Prestieri, along with the stellar Indigo Film team, Marica Gungui and Federica Felice. For more than ten years you have believed in these girls, and never gave up on them, and never gave up on me: thank you. To the wonderful directors Cosima Spender and Valerio Bonelli, who agreed in a second and a half to join us in this obsession, and make it their own: thank you.

To Leo and Elia, my loves, life with you is a glorious double backflip with three twists – crazy – but my favourite of them all. Thank you. One body. One heart.